TANNER TIMES TWO

A TANNER NOVEL - BOOK 11

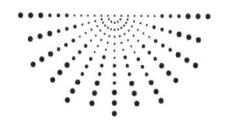

REMINGTON KANE

INTRODUCTION

TANNER TIMES TWO – A TANNER NOVEL – BOOK 11

Tanner and Alexa travel to Mexico with an unexpected ally, as they seek revenge against Alonso Alvarado.

However, Alvarado, the drug cartel leader, has hundreds of men to protect him.

Will Tanner defeat incredible odds once again, or will Alvarado triumph and see Tanner dead?

ACKNOWLEDGMENTS

I write for you.

—Remington Kane

PART I
ALLIES & ENEMIES

1

GOOD

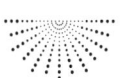

While stopped at a rest area on I-70 West in Kansas, near the Colorado border, Tanner realized that the three men standing by a soda machine were staring at him.

He was with Alexa and had been waiting for her to exit the ladies' room when he saw a guy in a blue work shirt nudge the man beside him and whisper something.

The man who was nudged turned and looked at Tanner; that was followed by the third man in the group turning to gaze his way as well.

When the first man took a piece of paper from his pocket, unfolded it, studied it, and then looked back at him, Tanner knew he had just been made.

He had already used the men's room, and it had been empty when he left it. It would be a good place to handle the three men and not make a public scene.

He also wanted to lure them away from Alexa and hoped that she wouldn't leave the ladies' room before he could take care of the men.

Tanner was five feet from the bathroom door when a teenager cut in front of him and went in first. The dark-haired kid was about eighteen and was Tanner's height. He wore a blue and orange knit cap with a matching football jersey that declared he was a fan of the Denver Broncos. Like Tanner, he was wearing jeans.

A quick glance back told Tanner that the men had decided to head his way, and with the kid involved, he had to change his plan. Once he'd entered the bathroom, Tanner yanked the cap off the kid's head and stuck a gun in his face.

"You do exactly what I say and you won't be hurt, understand?"

The boy looked angry, but the sight of the gun calmed him. He nodded as a look of fear entered his eyes.

"Good," Tanner said. "Take off the jersey, walk into the last stall, and sit down. Do it quick."

The kid was out of the football jersey in a flash and Tanner put it on over his own shirt as he watched the kid go into the stall.

"Stay quiet, kid, and you'll be all right."

Tanner had just enough time to move over in front of a urinal before the three men entered. He pretended to be urinating as he bobbed his head and hummed a tune.

Meanwhile, he was using the shiny metal of the flushing apparatus above the urinal to keep track of the men. He couldn't make out many details of them in the distorting reflective surface, but he could see their movements.

As Tanner hoped they would, the men saw the knit cap and matching jacket and took him for the kid. They then began peering under the doors of the stalls. When the man who had first spotted him took out a knife and headed for the stall the kid was in, Tanner made his move.

He was holding a metal baton. The type that telescoped out to its full length once you flicked your wrist to open it. The men's eyes were glued to the stall where the kid sat. They stiffened with surprise as they heard the baton snap into its full length, but they were too late to do anything about it.

Tanner caught two of them on the back of their skulls with his first swing. That stunned one man, while knocking the other unconscious. When the third man turned around, the man holding the knife, Tanner landed a blow on his face and broke his jaw.

The man bellowed from the pain and attempted to stab Tanner in the leg, but a third swing silenced him, while a backhanded movement with the baton knocked out the man who had only been stunned.

They were all out cold, but they would live. Spenser had convinced Tanner that, if possible, they shouldn't kill unless they had no choice. They were headed to Spenser's home in Wyoming. They didn't need to leave a trail of bodies for the cops or anyone else to follow them there.

The violent activity made Tanner's injured ribs ache. He leaned against the wall, after retrieving the knife the first man had dropped. It was a good blade, with razor sharp steel and a G-10 grip. Alexa would love it.

When the kid peeked his head out of the stall, Tanner told him to come out and walk over to him.

The boy's eyes were wide with wonder as he stared down at the three injured men. Tanner wiggled out of the jersey and handed it back to the kid along with the cap.

"Hey, were those guys after you?" the kid asked.

"Yeah," Tanner said.

The kid grinned. "You sure taught them a lesson."

Tanner took out his wallet, counted out three-hundred dollars, and handed it to the kid.

"Sorry about the gun in your face. Take your girl to a game on me."

The kid laughed. "Are you serious?"

"Yes," Tanner said, then he heard Alexa call his name through the door. When he opened the bathroom door, Alexa saw the three men sprawled out on the tile floor.

"Are you all right?" she asked.

"I'm good."

The kid looked Alexa up and down and his eyes widened with desire. "Hi."

Alexa smiled. "Hello. Did you help my friend?"

"No, but I let him wear my football jersey, so he could fool those guys."

"That sounds like help, and don't tell anyone you saw us, okay?"

"I won't," the kid said, but his eyes were locked on Alexa's breasts.

A man walked toward them. He had the look of someone who needed a bathroom and needed it immediately. As he moved past Alexa, he stopped short when he saw the three men on the bathroom floor.

The kid pointed at the men. "They were like that when we got here; I guess they had a fight."

The man hesitated for a second and then went inside. "I don't care. I have to go now."

As the man headed into a stall, Tanner and Alexa walked toward the exit with the kid tagging along beside them.

Tanner thought the boy must have entered the bathroom to pee, but with all the excitement the urge had apparently left him or been forgotten. Once they were outside, the kid pointed to a red Jeep with a blonde girl sitting in the passenger seat. Like the boy, she was dressed in Denver Bronco attire.

She called to him, as she looked Alexa over. "Who are they, Billy?"

Billy held up the money and tossed a thumb at Tanner. "I made a new friend, Cindy."

Tanner twitched slightly upon hearing their names, and Alexa took notice.

"Is something wrong?"

"No, just a memory surfacing. I once knew another Billy and Cindy, and they were about their age."

Tanner and Alexa told the kids goodbye and began walking toward her van. The boy drove past them, and he and the girl blew the horn, smiled, and waved.

Alexa decided to drive, and they were back on the road and headed toward Spenser Hawke's home in Wyoming. Tanner needed time to heal, and although Spenser had a plan to kill Alonso Alvarado, certain preparations had to be made in advance to carry it out.

Alexa looked over at Tanner. "Did you hurt your ribs?"

"A little, but it'll pass."

"How far ahead do you think Spenser and Amy are?"

"No more than an hour; we'll be at his place before nightfall."

Spenser knew that Tanner might find trouble like the three men left behind in the bathroom. He'd wanted to keep Amy away from any harm by driving on ahead.

Although Spenser was wanted by Alvarado, his eye patch helped him to avoid detection by anyone looking at the wanted poster with his face on it, a face that showed a man with two good eyes.

Alvarado had been looking for him for well over a decade. It seemed unlikely that he would be identified now. However, that assumption was a mistake, because the Tin Horsemen were headed to Spenser's house, and they would be there to greet his arrival.

Alexa sped the van along. "I want to get closer to Spenser and Amy."

"Why?"

Alexa turned her head and looked at Tanner. "I just feel like we should."

"You sense something?"

"Yes… something, but I'm not sure what."

"All right, we'll get closer, but don't speed too much. We don't need to attract a cop."

"What is Spenser's home like?"

"Very nice, and I helped him build it, along with Romeo."

"You're handy with tools?"

"Yeah, basic carpentry, some plumbing and electrical too."

"I hope he has a tub. I want to soak in sudsy water and relax."

"There's a huge tub in each room… and they're each big enough for two."

Alexa grinned. "That sounds like heaven."

Tanner looked at her as she drove. Alexa had come into his life at a time when he thought the last thing he wanted was a relationship, but after only spending a few days with her, he knew he wanted more of her.

Alexa felt his gaze. "What?"

"Nothing," he said.

She sent him a smile. "I feel it too."

"Feel what?"

"Good, I feel good when I'm near you."

"Yes," Tanner said, and then they grew silent as they rolled along the highway.

2

SEEDS OF BETRAYAL

The former Tin Horsemen, who had taken the place of the Hexalcorp Strike Team, were closing in on Spenser Hawke's home in Cody, Wyoming.

They were following a tip that Spenser was the man who had nearly killed Alonso Alvarado years ago, but didn't expect it to amount to anything, because they had learned that Spenser had only one eye.

Bruise, who was pretending to be Simms, drove, while Scar sat in the passenger seat beside him, and Wound and Abrasion rode in the rear.

The trip to Wyoming had taken a day longer than it should have, because Martinez had called and told them to gather their passports in case he needed them to leave the country in pursuit of Tanner.

Scar had called his mother and asked her to go out to their garage apartment where the boys lived, and to gather their passports. They all had valid passports, because of a previous trip they had taken to Canada the year before. Once the passports arrived by overnight mail, they were back on the road.

Scar kept staring at the drawing of Spenser. He was more certain than ever that he knew the man depicted in the sketch.

"I can't remember where and when it happened, but I've seen this guy before."

Abrasion leaned forward to look over Scar's shoulder. "Try to remember where you saw him, because the guy is worth a lot of money."

"I am trying, but I keep drawing a blank."

There was a GPS unit built into the truck that had taken them to the general vicinity of Spenser's home, but they had to rely on directions from the source of the tip as to where the house was actually located.

Scar had written the final directions on the back of the drawing of Spenser's face; he instructed Bruise to make a left down a private driveway.

Once they had made the turn, they ran along for about a thousand yards and could see Spenser's home growing nearer.

Wound spoke up from the back seat. "That's a nice place, and it's all out here on its own."

"We should be careful," Abrasion said. "If this is the home of the guy that Martinez wants us to find, that means he's dangerous."

Scar told Bruise to approach the house slowly. Bruise did so, and soon they were parked in front of the home.

"I don't see any cars," Wound said.

Scar opened his door and stepped out. "I'll go ring the bell."

"What if the guy in the drawing is inside?" Bruise said.

"Then we drive off and let Martinez know about it," Scar said, as he closed his door and headed for the front porch.

In Mexico, at the compound belonging to Alonso Alvarado, Martinez paced back and forth near the inner gate. With Tanner still on the loose, Alvarado had decided that he needed even more men sent out to patrol the desert. Martinez watched the men leave as several men returned from an earlier patrol.

When his phone rang, Martinez jumped slightly. He knew without looking that it was Alvarado calling him for news, and he had none to give.

"Yes sir, how may I help you?"

"I see you there by the gate watching the men enter and leave, tell me, should we begin using passwords?"

"Passwords?"

"Yes. What if Tanner entered while pretending to be one of the guards? If he didn't know the password, he would be found out."

"We could do that, but I have the men working in groups of two or three. If a single man attempted to enter the compound, he would be stopped."

"Ah, that's good, but begin using passwords as well. We have to keep Tanner from entering the compound."

"I'll get right on that," Martinez said, as he hoped that was all Alvarado wanted to discuss. It wasn't, and Alvarado asked him another question.

"Tell me, have you heard any news from your strike team?"

"No sir, but I am expecting some soon. With Tanner laying low, I've instructed them to follow another lead. It concerns the man who attacked you years ago."

"That bastard! I think I still want him more than I want Tanner. Deliver that man to me, Martinez, and I'll give you anything you want."

"I hope to do so, along with Tanner and the woman."

"The woman, is she really working with Tanner?"

"It appears so."

"Find them, Martinez, my patience is growing short."

"Yes sir."

When the call ended, Martinez pulled up the sketch of Alexa on his phone. Tanner had no one who could be threatened to make him come forth, but what about the woman? If they could find out who she was, they could then find her family and use them to draw her out, and possibly force her to choose between her loved ones and Tanner.

Tanner trusted the woman, or he wouldn't be working with her. That trust made him vulnerable. If they could find out who she was, they might have a way to control her, to make her betray Tanner.

Martinez headed toward the house to talk to Alvarado in person. He had just thought of a way to kill two birds with one stone.

3
BREAK-IN

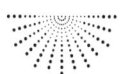

Once they were certain that no one was at home, Scar, Bruise, Wound, and Abrasion went around Spenser's house looking for an unlocked door or window.

They found that everything was locked up tight, but while walking along the roof that sat over the wraparound porch, Scar gazed through a bedroom window and saw a picture on a nightstand that caught his attention.

It was a photo of Spenser and Amy, and when Scar compared it to the drawing he had, he realized that Spenser was a good match. He also remembered where and when he had seen Spenser before.

Knowing that he had to be sure he was right, Scar climbed down from the roof, walked to the rear door that led into the kitchen, and smashed a pane of glass by using his elbow. As he reached in through the hole to undo the lock on the door, Bruise, Abrasion, and Wound gawked at him.

"Dude, what are you doing?" Bruise said.

Scar ignored him, opened the door, and moved through the house. The others followed him upstairs to the bedroom, where he lifted up the picture of Spenser and Amy and studied it.

"It's him," Scar said. "It's really him."

∿

Miles away, Spenser pulled his truck over to the side of the road as his phone emitted a strange tone.

"What's that noise?" Amy asked.

"It's the burglar alarm for my house. I think someone may have broken in."

"Your alarm sends a signal to your phone?"

"Yeah, and it's new. Roger Trask installed the alarm system just a week ago."

"Trask? He was a client, wasn't he?"

"Yes, and he installed new alarms as a way of saying thank you, and now I wish I had let him install cameras as well. For all I know a tree branch could have broken a window."

"What do you want to do?"

Spenser put his truck in gear and pulled back into traffic. "We're almost there, so I'll check it out."

"But if someone has broken in, they'll hear the truck before we reach the house. You know how well sound carries out there."

"I do, which is why you'll stay with the truck while I go in on foot."

"Maybe we should call Tanner and Alexa and wait for them to catch up to us."

"They're probably too far back, and I can handle anything I find."

Amy let out a worried sigh. "It's times like this that I feel useless."

"You're far from useless, and when we get to Mexico we'll be counting on you."

"You really think that plan of yours will work?"

"I do, honey, and then Cody and Alexa will be safe."

"You're wanted by that man Alvarado too. Do you think this break-in could have something to do with that?"

"I don't know," Spenser said, as he pressed down harder on the truck's gas pedal.

∽

AT THE HOUSE, SCAR AND HIS MEN HAD MOVED DOWN TO the living room, where he took a seat on a leather sofa with Bruise, as Abrasion and Wound sat across from them on a matching love seat.

Scar held up the picture of Spenser and Amy, then he looked at each of the others in turn.

"This guy in the picture, he's the one that saved my mom and me after my dad was killed."

"Seriously?" Wound said.

"No shit," Scar said. "And I know he's worth a lot of money if we tell Martinez where he is, but I ain't gonna do it."

"Dude, he's worth a *lot* of money," Abrasion said.

Scar looked over at him with an uncharacteristic steely gaze, then stood to walk over and glare down at him. "This dude is off-limits. Do you hear me?"

Abrasion nodded in agreement. "I get it. You owe him; I was just sayin', that's all."

Bruise raised a hand in the air as if he were in school and trying to get a teacher's attention. When Scar looked at him, he spoke.

"You didn't tell us much back when all that shit went

down, but dude, if we're gonna pass up the kind of money this guy is worth, I want to know why."

When both Abrasion and Wound echoed Bruise's request, Scar began pacing in front of the fireplace.

"I'll tell you, but you can't tell anyone else."

The boys agreed, and Scar began telling them about Spenser Hawke.

~

Spenser left the truck a short time later and grabbed a rifle from the rear. He was parked along the side of the road about a mile from his house. Before leaving, he spoke to Amy.

"I'll call you when I know it's safe to come up. If you don't get that call, do not come near the house."

"Maybe I should come with you."

"No, honey, it may be dangerous."

"But how long should I wait?"

"Let's say an hour, and then you drive into town, and call Cody and Alexa too."

Amy kissed Spenser. "Be careful."

"I will."

Spenser cut through the trees and began jogging toward his home in a direction that would let him come upon it from the right side. The house sat in the open with only a few trees strategically planted to give shade. There was no way to approach it without the risk of being spotted.

While still some distance away, Spenser moved forward in a crouch. He soon dropped down and lay flat, as he brought up the rifle and peered through the scope. Through a living room window, he could see Scar as he stood by the fireplace talking, but he couldn't get a clear view of his face.

Spenser stayed like that for several minutes and wondered just how many men were in the house. Unless Scar was prone to talking to himself, he knew it had to be at least two, but given how Scar's gaze swiveled right, then left, he thought it a safer bet to assume that there were three or four people inside.

Having only one eye, Spenser had developed the habit of checking any reflective surface in his immediate area that could reveal movement on his blind side, his left side. That's why he spotted the shapes coming up behind him. They were reflected on the surface of the wide silver band he wore on his wrist.

Spenser released the unwieldy rifle, rolled to his right, and reached for the gun beneath his jacket.

4

TURN AROUND

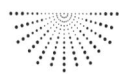

"It was back when we were thirteen, remember?" Scar said. "That was the year my dad walked in on that bank robbery."

Bruise, Abrasion, and Wound nodded. They had been friends with Scar since the third grade, and they remembered well the period that Scar spoke of.

"The cops never caught those guys, did they?" Bruise said.

Scar shook his head. "The cops didn't get them, but the guy in the picture did."

Bruise held up the photo of Spenser and Amy. "This guy? He helped you and your mom?"

"Yeah, and I never said anything to you guys because I knew you would talk. I mean, we were kids, and I knew you would've told everyone in school... if you knew what really happened."

Abrasion stood and walked over to Scar. "Hey man, we ain't kids no more, and you know you can tell us anything, right?"

Scar smiled. "Yeah, and to tell you the truth, I don't

know much, but I think the guy with the eye patch killed the bank robbers."

"The dudes that killed your father? He killed all three of them? But I thought the cops said the guys got away," Bruise said.

Scar shook his head slowly. "My dad saw one of the robbers without his mask and recognized the guy. The dude was an ex-cop. Dad didn't die right away, and he told my mom the guy's name when she saw him in the hospital."

"Your mom gave the dude's name to the cops?" Bruise asked.

"After my dad died, Mom was too scared to go to the police, since one of the bank robbers used to be one of them. So, we drove off to see a friend of hers that lived here in Wyoming. Her friend contacted this guy with the eye patch, and he said he would help. I was just a kid then, you know, just thirteen, so nobody told me much. But I know he killed them, because a few days after he showed up, my mom told me that I never had to worry about them ever again."

Bruise stood. "If this guy is as tough as you think he is maybe we should leave."

"No," Scar said. "I've got to see him again. The dude saved my life, and my mom's life too, plus, I think we should tell him about Martinez and the reward that they're offering for him."

Abrasion was holding the picture; he ran a finger over Amy's face. "This lady is so pretty. If Martinez sent men here, they might hurt her too. We can't let that happen."

Wound stood and walked over to join Scar. "Talk to the guy if you want to, but we should wait in the truck. If he catches us in here he might shoot us."

Scar thought that over and agreed. "Yeah, we'll wait

outside, and I hope he's not pissed about me breaking in, but I had to know if it was really him."

"What if he don't come back for days?" Wound said.

"Then we wait," Scar said. "But I got a feeling he'll be here soon."

∽

Spenser was bringing his gun up to take aim when he realized it was Tanner and Alexa coming toward him.

"Damn Cody, how did you two get here so quickly?"

Tanner tossed a thumb toward Alexa. "She had a feeling that there might be trouble and we've been moving fast since leaving Kansas."

Spenser grinned at Alexa. "I'm taking you to Vegas someday and see how you do at a craps table."

Alexa laughed. "I've tried gambling and I always lose. I don't think my gift approves of me getting something for nothing."

Tanner settled on the ground on Spenser's right, as Alexa lowered herself beside Tanner.

"What's up?" Tanner asked. "Amy said that someone might have broken in."

Spenser was staring through the scope again, and this time he could make out Wound, Abrasion, and Bruise, along with Scar.

"There's at least four of them, and they look young."

Alexa held out her hand. "May I borrow that rifle scope? I want to check out that pickup truck they arrived in."

Spenser passed her the rifle, and after sighting in on the truck, Alexa looked at Tanner. "That's the same truck that those men who were after you were using. Maybe these four are their replacements."

Tanner took the rifle from her. After staring through the scope at the truck, he looked at the men, and recognized them as the Tin Horsemen.

"Those four are the bikers that attacked you at the motel in Oklahoma City, Alexa. Spenser, we need to take them alive. I think they have answers we need."

Spenser was about to reply when all three of them heard someone approaching from behind. When they looked, they saw Amy.

"Why aren't you waiting in the truck?" Spenser said.

"I'm tired of sitting in the truck," Amy said, as she settled beside Alexa.

Spenser let out a sigh. "I don't know why I expected you to do as I asked, you never have before."

"What's going on?" Amy said, and after Alexa explained, Amy had a question.

"How are you going to approach them without being spotted?"

Tanner rubbed his chin. "We need a distraction. If they're all busy looking left, we can come up on them from the right."

Amy smiled. "I can help. I'm not good with a gun, but I can be distracting."

"How?" Spenser said.

Amy stood and began walking toward the house. "You'll see, now get ready."

Spenser reached for her hand to bring her back, but Amy was already out of reach.

"That woman," Spenser whispered in an exasperated tone, then he looked over and saw that Tanner and Alexa were smiling.

"It's not funny. She could get hurt."

Tanner moved toward the rear of the house. "Let's make sure she stays safe."

~

Scar left the house by the front door with the others following. They were about to climb in the truck to wait, when Bruise raised an arm and pointed out by the generator shed, which was about a hundred feet from the house.

"Look, a lady."

It was Amy. She was wearing a blue skirt with a yellow top; as the boys watched, she began unbuttoning her blouse.

"What's she doing?" Wound asked. "Is she... is she taking off her top?"

Abrasion's mouth hung open as he watched Amy. "It's the lady from the picture... she's beautiful."

Amy teased them for several moments as she slowly removed the blouse to reveal a black lace bra. Scar and his men watched enraptured as Amy smiled, turned her back on them, undid the bra's clasps, and then took it off.

"Turn around," Abrasion said softly, as he and the others kept staring at Amy.

She turned with her arms covering her breasts and smiled at the boys. "If you have any weapons on you, I wouldn't reach for them."

Scar had been staring intently at her as he tried to glimpse something more than Amy's arms and her taut stomach. When her words finally penetrated his brain, he asked a question.

"What are you talking about?"

"Look behind you," Amy said.

Scar and the others turned, and when they saw Tanner and Spenser pointing weapons at them, they raised their hands in the air.

"Who are you?" Spenser asked.

When Spenser received no answer, Tanner stepped closer to Scar, who was the tallest of the boys. He aimed his gun at his head.

"Don't shoot!" Scar said.

Tanner pressed his gun against Scar's forehead. "Give me a reason not to."

Scar shifted his eyes over to Spenser, just as Amy came to stand at Spenser's side while fastening her blouse.

"I know you, and you know me too. I'm Mary Fenwick's son."

Spenser recalled the name and lowered his weapon. "You're Johnny Fenwick?"

"Yeah, but they call me Scar now."

Alexa had been inside the house looking for more intruders. When she came back outside, she walked over to check out the vehicle.

"I see guns on the dashboard, and they broke in through the kitchen door."

After opening the truck, she began removing the weapons, and when she came across them, she held up the wanted posters with their faces on them.

"Whoever he is, he and his friends were hunting us."

After placing the weapons on the porch steps, Alexa walked over to Bruise and kicked his feet out from under him. Before Bruise knew what was happening, Alexa had a knife at his throat, as she looked up at Scar.

"Tell us who you work for or I'll kill him."

Scar held out a hand. A hand that displayed the healing cut from his first encounter with Alexa.

"Whoa! Whoa! Chill, we're on your side. Well, we are now, and all I know is that the dude who sent us here is named Robert Martinez and he works for something called Hexalcorp."

Tanner and Spenser looked at each other.

"Why would a corporation be sending people out to look for you, Spenser?" Amy asked.

Alexa removed her knife from Bruise's throat and stood. "It's Alvarado. He must have hired Hexalcorp to help locate us. They have resources that he doesn't."

Tanner removed his gun from Scar's forehead. "You need to tell us everything you know."

Scar nodded, as he pointed at Spenser. "We will, I owe him."

Tanner, Amy, and Alexa looked at Spenser, and Spenser explained. "His mother was one of my clients years ago. If I hadn't been called in, he and his mother would be dead."

Alexa spoke to Scar. "Is there anyone else on the way here?"

"No, Martinez just told us to check it out, but he didn't sound like he thought we would find anything."

"That sounds about right," Tanner said. "If they knew Spenser was here for certain, they would have sent more than these four to check things out."

Amy began walking back toward the spot where she'd left Spenser's truck. "I'll get the truck while you sort through this."

Abrasion rushed to her side and pointed back toward the pickup. "I could give you a lift."

Amy stopped walking and looked at him. Abrasion was only an inch taller than she was, and his brown hair was shoulder-length. He wore a goofy smile and his eyes were staring at her breasts.

"I'm not taking my top off again if that's what you're thinking."

Abrasion took a step back as he shook his head. "I was just trying to be nice."

Alexa walked over to them. "You'll drive us both, and if you try anything, you'll be sorry."

Abrasion scowled at her. "You kicked me in the balls the last time I saw you, and they still hurt."

Alexa gave him a shove. "Just drive where we tell you to go."

Tanner called to her. "Keep him with you when you drive your van back here."

"Right, and when we return we'll figure out our next move."

"Yes," Tanner said, and he smiled at her. He'd been doing that a lot lately it seemed.

Alexa smiled back at him as she sent him a wink, then she and Amy went to retrieve their vehicles.

5

MAKING PLANS

After Amy and Alexa returned with the vehicles, they found that Spenser had thrown two frozen pizzas in the oven. Scar and the other Tin Horsemen were seated on stools in front of the kitchen island, awaiting the meal.

Tanner saw Alexa frown at the Horsemen, and he told Abrasion to join his friends on the stools.

"Maybe we should tie them up," Alexa said.

"Spenser doesn't think it's necessary and neither do I," Tanner said. "But if any of them do something stupid, they'll wish they hadn't."

"We just want to help," Scar said.

"You can help by telling us what you know," Spenser said. "How did you come to be here?"

Scar told them about finding the original Hexalcorp Strike Team dead at the house in Oklahoma City, and the details of Martinez' call.

Alexa laughed. "He hoped to pass you four off as an elite team of mercenaries? The man must be desperate."

"He is," Tanner said. "If he told Alvarado that his men failed, he'd probably be killed. I'm going to call my contact at the Burke Corporation. He might know something about this man Martinez, and he'll also give me the latest satellite images of Alvarado's compound."

"Do that," Spenser said. "The more info we have, the better."

~

When the pizza was ready, Amy reached up into a cupboard for glasses. She had grabbed two of them, and when she reached back to get more, she saw that Abrasion had moved over to help her. As he handed her more glasses, she asked him his name.

"I'm Abrasion."

"That can't be your real name."

Abrasion shook his head. "Nope, my real name is Lionel."

"Thank you for helping me, Lionel," Amy said, and Abrasion blushed.

~

As everyone sat around eating pizza and drinking soda, Spenser and Tanner asked the boys more questions, as they tried to come up with a plan that would throw suspicion off Spenser while satisfying Martinez and Alvarado.

Tanner needed time to heal and there were preparations to make before they made their assault on Alvarado's compound. After listening to the conversation, Alexa said she had an idea.

"Let's hear it," Spenser said.

"I'll contact Damián Sandoval and ask for help. He has much to gain from Alvarado's downfall."

"What sort of help?" Tanner said.

"His cartel extends into Texas, as does Alvarado's cartel. It would be a simple thing for him to make Alvarado's people believe you were in the state and causing havoc."

"You mean have his people kill Alvarado's people and claim that I did it? That sounds like a big favor," Tanner said.

"Maybe," Alexa said. "But I think he'll do it. I also think he'll support us once we get inside Mexico."

"That would be invaluable," Spenser said. "How will you make contact?"

"They gave me a laptop with a Skype connection. I'll be contacting Sandoval's man, Dante."

"After I make this call to my contact at Burke, I'll need to buy a new phone," Tanner said. "I shouldn't risk using the one I have much longer."

"I keep a few throwaway phones for use in my work," Spenser said. "I'll give you one of those."

Amy stood and began grabbing the empty paper plates and glasses, over at the kitchen island, Abrasion did the same, then he stood next to Amy as she leaned back against the sink.

"I have a call to make too, Spenser," Amy said. "You know, the things we'll need for your plan."

"How long will it take to get that stuff here?" Spenser asked.

"I'll have them ship it overnight, but I'll need time to get it just right."

"Get what right?" Scar said.

"Don't worry about it," Alexa said, as she still didn't trust Scar and the others.

∽

While Spenser kept watch over the Tin Horsemen, Tanner, Alexa, and Amy each went off to make calls and talk to their contacts.

After sending off a message to Dan Matthews of the Burke Corporation, Tanner was surprised to receive an email back only a minute later. The email contained a phone number and a request to call as soon as possible. Tanner had expected Matthews to call him on the phone they had previously used, but knew the man was a stickler for security, so he used one of Spenser's throwaway phones.

Tanner called Matthews immediately, and heard the man answer after only one ring.

"Tanner?"

"It's me, Matthews, what's so urgent?"

"Hold on, Mr. Burke wants to speak to you."

When Conrad Burke came on the line, Tanner recognized the man's voice from the times they had seen each other in Guambi.

"It's me, Burke, what's up?"

"I need a favor from you, Tanner."

"I'm listening."

"It concerns Robert Martinez of Hexalcorp. Your email stated that he was inside Alonso Alvarado's compound. Are you certain of that?"

"I can't be certain, but that's the information I have."

Tanner heard a sigh come through the phone line; it was followed by Burke speaking. "I need to keep Martinez alive, the damn fool."

"I take it you know him?"

"Unfortunately, he was once married to my wife's sister and they share a child, which I suppose makes him family."

"All right, I won't kill him unless I have to, but I can't speak for what Alvarado might do to him."

"How did you come to learn that Robert was inside the compound?"

Tanner told Burke about the Hexalcorp Strike Team and Martinez's attempt to use the Tin Horsemen as their replacements, to deceive Alvarado.

"Robert is an idiot. When those men fail to get results Alvarado will be furious with him."

"Maybe not, we have a plan forming that will make it seem as if they're making progress. It may buy Martinez more time."

"Fine, but Tanner, what's your ultimate plan? Alvarado is being guarded by an army of men, too many for even you to kill all of them."

"For one thing, I won't be alone, there are three of us."

"Three?" Burke said, in a voice that was filled with disbelief. "Tanner, if you had three hundred helping you it might not be enough. My analysts have studied the satellite photos we've taken of the compound and Alvarado has beefed up his security tremendously. My people tell me that there's absolutely no way for you to enter that compound, and that any attempt would leave you dead."

"I guess we'll see, Burke."

"You have nothing to lose by the attempt; I can see that, given that Alvarado won't rest until you're dead."

"That's right."

"I guess there's nothing else to say except to wish you luck, and if by some miracle you do kill Alvarado, my job offer still stands."

"Good, as long as you remember that I'll remain an independent."

"I understand, and good luck."

Burke ended the call, and, after checking, Tanner saw that he had a new email. When he opened it, he found a set of detailed satellite maps that displayed the Alvarado compound.

He was impressed. Working for Burke could have advantages when it came to intel, and when planning a hit, accurate information about a target could make all the difference between success or failure. Tanner pushed Burke from his mind and thought about Alonso Alvarado, a man he wanted to kill more than any other.

"I'm coming, Alvarado," he whispered, and then he went off to find Alexa.

6
ATROCITY

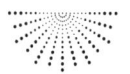

Alexa had moved onto the porch with her laptop to contact Damián Sandoval's man, Dante Cardoso.

When the connection went through, she saw Dante's mustached face smiling back at her. Dante knew her as Anna Sanchez. He looked genuinely pleased to hear from her.

"Anna, it's good to see you, and I hope this means you have news."

"I do. I've found Tanner and the two of us will be coming back to Mexico in a few days."

"Why the delay?"

"Tanner has injuries that need to heal first, but once we reach Mexico, we'll be headed straight for Alvarado's compound."

Dante laughed. "If you do that you'll be slaughtered before you reach the gates. Alvarado has tightened security and hired more guards. In fact, you now have to pass through two separate gates to enter the place."

Alexa cocked her head. "How could you know all that? Does Sandoval have another spy inside?"

All traces of humor left Dante's face. When he spoke again, there was the sound of sadness in his voice.

"Do you remember Joaquin?"

"The young guard you let live? Yes, of course I remember him."

"He got word to me. I must have slipped once and told him about a bar in Mexico City that I liked to drink in. He left a message for me there, and I met him outside the compound while he was out on a patrol. After you breached the compound, Alvarado expanded the perimeter guard. Now there are men on patrol nearly a mile out."

"So, Joaquin switched sides?" Alexa asked. "Did he say why?"

On the laptop screen, Dante nodded his head slowly. "It was the whores. The ones that were brought in the night you breached the compound. In order to maintain the belief that the compound was impenetrable… Alvarado ordered them all killed, to silence them."

Alexa blinked rapidly, as her stomach roiled. "He… he killed those women… because of me?"

"No!" Dante shouted. "Alvarado killed those women because he is a monster. And while he managed to keep news of the breach from spreading, he also turned the local people against him. Those women were whores, yes, but they were also sisters, daughters, and some were even young mothers."

Alexa covered her mouth with her hands, while fearing she might be sick.

"Poor Joaquin," Dante said. "He was one of the men sent out to dig the graves. He was forced to watch the slaughter as well. He has no more love for Alvarado after witnessing that, and he's been giving us news from inside the compound."

Alexa took several deep breaths, wiped away tears, and asked another question.

"How does Joaquin make contact? Do you still meet him in the desert?"

"No, there are too many men with scoped rifles checking the desert now, but Joaquin found a cell phone in the room that was Carlos Ayala's; he uses it to make contact."

"What has he told you?"

"There is an American helping Alvarado, a man named—"

"—Martinez," Alexa said, and watched as Dante arched an eyebrow in surprise.

"How do you know about Martinez?"

"Tanner and I have our own spies, and we also have a new ally. This ally is the same man who crippled Alvarado years ago."

"Ah, you are full of surprises, Anna, and I will tell Sandoval what you have told me. I think he may be willing to lend assistance."

"That's good, because we need a favor."

"And what would that be?" Dante said.

Alexa told him about their plan to make Alvarado believe that she and Tanner were in Texas.

"I think Sandoval will go for it. In any event, there's a man in the West End area of Dallas that we need to eliminate."

"Thank you," Alexa said. "And the sooner the better."

"Anna?"

"Yes?"

"You're not to blame for what Alvarado did to those whores, you know that, right?"

"All I know is that there are more deaths that I owe

Alvarado for, and the day is coming when I'll make him pay."

Alexa ended the call and turned off her laptop. Afterwards, she stood at the top of the porch steps and watched the Bighorn Mountains grow shadows and become less distinct as night grew closer.

When her mind turned again to the women that Alvarado had killed to keep her breach of his compound a secret, a wave of guilt came over her. It was followed by disgust, was given imagination, and she could almost feel the fear of those women as they knew they were about to die. She made it to a tree near the side of the house before her stomach betrayed her, and she vomited.

Alvarado was a monster in human form. If it cost Alexa her very life, she knew she would give it gladly to kill the man.

She grabbed a breath mint from the cup holder in her van, straightened her clothes, and went back inside the house to talk to Tanner.

7
CHEAT SHEET

Alvarado agreed with Martinez' plan to place more emphasis on finding out who Alexa really was. Once they knew her identity, they could then use her loved ones against her, and hopefully persuade her to betray Tanner.

Martinez was with Alvarado inside the man's office as he discussed the search with Alvarado and Alvarado's wife, Malena. Malena studied the drawing of Alexa and made an observation to Martinez.

"If this drawing is accurate, she's not very old," Malena said. "We should have someone check the schools and colleges. Maybe a teacher will recognize her. You can say you're looking for her because of an inheritance."

Martinez smiled in agreement. "Yes, that's a good idea, and we'll concentrate on Mexico City."

"And what are you doing about finding Tanner?" Alvarado said. "I thought that damn strike team of yours would have tracked him down by now."

"If you'll recall, I sent them to search for the other man you're after. I should be hearing back from them soon on that."

Alvarado made a face of disgust. "I hate that man even more than I hate Tanner, but I've nearly given up on finding the son of a bitch."

Martinez smiled, and his even white teeth broadcast sincerity. "At Hexalcorp we never give up, and we will never stop until you're satisfied."

Malena balled up the drawing of Alexa and tossed it at Martinez. It smacked him in the face and made him flinch. When Martinez looked over at her, he saw the fury in her eyes.

"We don't want sound-bites or slogans, Mr. Martinez—we want results. Maybe my husband is willing to give you more time, but my patience has ended. Find the woman who killed my brother or find Tanner, but if you make another false promise in my presence you'll regret it."

Malena left the room without saying another word. When Martinez looked over at Alvarado, he saw that he was staring at him.

"Maybe you should call your strike team and tell them the situation here. It looks like your time is about up."

Martinez took out his phone and said a silent prayer that Scar would have good news for him.

∽

Scar jumped when the phone in his pocket rang, because he knew it was Martinez calling him for an update.

Tanner and Spenser had coached him on what to say and had even written several things down on a cheat sheet for Scar to refer to.

Scar looked nervously about the room as everyone stared back at him. When he answered the call, he placed it on the speakerphone setting so that the others could hear.

"Um, Bennett here," Scar said, while pitching his voice lower. He was pretending to be Steve Bennett, just in case Alvarado was also on speakerphone.

"This is Martinez, Bennett, along with the client. What's your status?"

Martinez use of the word, status, confused Scar, and Tanner reached over and pointed to one of the things written on the cheat sheet.

"Oh, we checked out that house in Cody, Wyoming. It was empty. There must have been a fire recently, because the place was gutted."

"What about the man that was living there?"

"We found people that knew him, and they all said that he matched the sketch."

"Excellent, and do you know where to find him now?"

"Yeah, we finally found him today, but uh, this guy, he looks like the sketch, yeah, but he's only about five feet tall."

"He's short?"

"Yeah, short and fat, and we asked around and people say that he doesn't have a brother."

The sound of Martinez cursing came over the speakerphone, and Tanner pointed to another line of words on the cheat sheet.

"We have new information on Tanner. A friend of mine says that he saw him in Texas. We're on our way there now."

Before Martinez could answer, a different voice could be heard, it was the voice of Alonso Alvarado. The voice was soft, but gruff, and spoke English with a strong Mexican accent.

"This is the client speaking. What part of Texas was Tanner spotted in?" Alvarado asked.

Tanner looked at Alexa and saw her flinch, even as her face darkened with anger, then he pointed at the sheet again, to give Scar his cue.

"Dallas," Scar said. "My buddy spotted him in the West End area."

This time it was Alvarado's turn to curse, and after doing so, he relayed news to Martinez, and his words carried over the phone.

"I received a call right before our meeting. The man who runs my distribution into Texas was shot to death in his West End apartment. I believed it was Sandoval's doing, but it must have been Tanner."

Martinez asked Scar a question. "Bennett, this friend of yours, did he see the woman, was she with Tanner?"

Scar searched the sheet and found nothing there that could help. When he looked up at Tanner, he saw him nod yes, and then hold up three fingers and point at Spenser.

"Um, yeah, the woman was with him… and so was someone else?"

Scar had phrased the answer as a question, because he was unsure what Tanner had meant by holding up three fingers, but when Tanner nodded his approval, Scar knew he had gotten it right.

"Tanner has two companions now?"

"Yeah… a man and a woman," Scar said, and again, Tanner nodded his approval.

An idea struck Spenser at that moment, and he rushed to Scar's side and whispered something in his ear.

"My friend managed to get a picture of the other man. I'll have him send you a copy."

"There's a picture?" Martinez said.

"Yeah, but just one."

"Call the man and have him send it now," Alvarado said.

"All right, and we're headed for Texas," Scar said, as he read from the cheat sheet. "That asshole Tanner is a dead man."

Martinez told Scar to forward the picture as soon as possible, then he ended the call.

After shutting his phone off, Scar looked up at Tanner.

"I wasn't calling you an asshole, dude; that's what was written on the sheet."

"I know," Tanner said. "I'm the one who wrote it, and you did good."

Spenser had opened his laptop and was looking through old photos. When he found one that was taken with Amy and only showed himself from the right side, he asked Amy if she could crop it and send it to one of the throwaway cell phones.

Amy was seated beside Spenser on a sofa; she slid the laptop over and went to work on the picture.

"This is one from our last trip to New Orleans."

"Right, and I need it cropped so that your face isn't showing."

Amy's fingers flew over the keyboard, in a short time, she had the picture cropped, then she sent it to a cell phone.

Abrasion smiled at her. "You know computers?"

"Just some basic stuff," Amy said, and Abrasion kept smiling at her.

Spenser snapped his fingers, breaking Abrasion's trance, and then held up the phone. "Hand that to Johnny."

"Who?"

"Scar, his real name is Johnny," Spenser said.

Abrasion took the phone, and walked it over to Scar, who then sent the photo to Martinez.

Alexa smiled. "Once Alvarado sees that photo he'll be twice as worried as he already is."

Tanner went over to her and brushed back her hair. "It was difficult to hear his voice again, wasn't it?"

"Yes, although I barely remember the sound of it. What fills my mind are the images of him killing my family."

Bruise appeared startled. "That dude Alvarado killed your family?"

Alexa nodded. She had been wary of the Horsemen, but she had come to see that they were a group of aimless boys and not hardened men.

Bruise looked over at Scar. "You were right to help them, and that dude Martinez must be a dirtbag too."

Wound let out a yawn, then he looked over at Spenser. "Can we crash in here tonight or do we have to sleep out in the truck?"

Amy stood. "There are blankets and pillows upstairs, along with a couple of sleeping bags. Between the sofa and the sleeping bags you'll be comfortable right here in the living room."

Amy headed for the stairs, and Abrasion followed her.

"I'll help you carry stuff."

Amy started to protest, but then shrugged. "Thank you, Lionel, I could use the help."

As Amy and Abrasion headed up the stairs, Tanner walked over to Spenser.

"Sending that picture was risky. Now, Alvarado will know you're still alive."

Spenser grinned. "That's right, and as soon as you're healed, we'll head straight for him."

"Give me two more days to let my ribs heal and I'll be ready."

"We'll all be ready," Alexa said. "And then Alvarado will die."

8

A TANNER NEVER FAILS

Try as he might, Alvarado couldn't keep his hand from shaking as he looked at the picture of Spenser Hawke.

The photo only showed Spenser from the right side, and he was more than a dozen years older than the last time Alvarado had seen him. However, his face was burned into Alvarado's memory. He knew right away that he was the man who had crippled him and left him for dead in Matamoros.

"It's him," Alvarado said to Martinez. "This is the bastard who attacked me years ago."

Martinez let out a sigh of relief as he stood before Alvarado's desk. His results so far had been less than stellar, thanks to Tanner and Alexa's destruction of his strike team. Now it looked as if his luck had changed, and he was going to make the most of it.

"How long have you been looking for that man?"

From where he sat in his special chair, Alvarado tore his eyes away from the photo and stared up at Martinez.

"Eighteen years, this bastard crippled me eighteen years ago."

"And now I've found him for you, and not only that, but we've also established that he has a link to Tanner. I think you'll agree that I've shown I can be valuable to you, yes?"

Alvarado let out a chuckle. "You've earned a reprieve, yes, but I want more. I want this man in the photo along with Tanner and the woman."

"I've already sent people to Dallas to track them down, and of course, my strike team is headed there as well. But it appears to me that Tanner has decided to adopt a plan of lashing out and then going into hiding. If that's true, he may not surface for a while. It would also mean that the three of them are still in Dallas, which is great news, because if they're there, we'll find them."

Alvarado held up Spenser's picture. "I'll take him dead, but if you can bring this man to me alive, I will give you anything you want, and I do mean anything."

Martinez' dark eyes flashed with pure avarice. "I'll do my best, sir, count on it."

∽

SPENSER LAY BESIDE AMY IN BED AND SET HIS ALARM FOR four a.m.

Although they believed that the Tin Horsemen were on their side and essentially harmless, they weren't yet ready to trust them fully. Spenser and Tanner were taking shifts on keeping watch throughout the night. After Spenser turned off the light, Amy snuggled against him.

"I really think it's unnecessary for you to get up early to keep an eye on those boys, they seem harmless," Amy said.

"I agree, but I'd hate to be wrong and wake up to find one of them standing over us with a knife."

"Lionel would never do something like that, and neither would the others."

"That kid, Abrasion, or Lionel as you call him, he'd like to stick you, but not with a knife."

Amy laughed and gave Spenser a playful punch on his arm. "Lionel's sweet, and yes, I think he has a crush on me."

"I'd better watch my back around him."

"I called my mother. She's going to send the things I need to the store, so tomorrow I'll go and pick them up after lunch."

"Why don't you ask that girl Deedee to bring them out here? It would save you a drive."

"I want to stop in and see my brother before we leave for Mexico, and besides, with me not there, he can really use Deedee's help at the store."

"It's not too late for you to back out of this, Amy. I don't think you'll be at risk in Mexico, but I also don't like the idea of you being anywhere near a man like Alvarado."

"No Spenser, I'll do my part, and anyway, you need me if your plan is to work."

"That's true, and I've tried to come up with another plan, but nothing seems as likely to work as the one I've already got."

Amy hugged him. "I'm so afraid for you. I know that you and Tanner are as deadly as they come, but you'll be going up against so many men."

"We'll survive. The plan will work, and we'll survive."

Amy kissed him. "I couldn't bear to lose you."

Spenser's hands slipped beneath her nightgown, and

soon all thoughts of pain and loss were replaced by those of pleasure.

∿

DOWNSTAIRS, ALEXA STOOD IN THE DOORWAY LEADING TO the living room and frowned as she looked at the Tin Horsemen, who were all asleep. She left them and walked into the kitchen, where she sat beside Tanner at the table.

"Those boys snore," she said.

"Which ones?"

"All of them, and I still don't know whether we can trust them or not."

"I don't either, but I also think they seem sincere. Like Scar said, he owes Spenser his life."

Alexa gazed around at the kitchen. "I like this house."

"Yeah, but I was surprised when Spenser said he wanted to settle in one spot. Up until we built this place he was always a wanderer."

"And you traveled with him for years?"

"Yes, both Romeo and I were young, and Spenser became a sort of surrogate father to us. Romeo's father was still alive then, but he never really got along with the man."

Alexa reached over and took Tanner's hand. "This plan of Spenser's is brilliant, but it's also risky. There's a chance that one of us won't make it. If I die… I just want you to know that I've come to care for you a great deal, even if we've only known each other a short time."

Tanner linked his fingers with hers. "I care for you too, Alexa."

Tanner leaned in and they kissed, when it ended, he gave her hand a gentle squeeze before releasing it.

"We'll survive. Never think about dying, only about killing. Dying takes care of itself, while killing takes thought and planning."

Alexa grinned. "You really are fearless."

"No, I'm not, but I do feel less fear than most, and I never let it control me. I'll die someday, like everyone else, and fearing it will make no difference at all. When Alvarado shot me and left me for dead, I should have died… the way my family died, but I lived, and every day since has been a gift."

"I feel the same way, but I'll never have peace until that man is dead."

Tanner placed a hand on her cheek. "You'll soon have peace, believe it."

Alexa stood and stretched. "I'm going to take a long bath and then go to bed, but I want you to wake me when you come up."

"You have plans for me?"

Alexa grinned. "I most certainly do."

She walked to the doorway, then turned and looked back at Tanner.

Tanner searched her eyes, saw the worry still lurking there, and then he smiled.

"We'll get through this in one piece. Remember something, Spenser and I are both Tanners, and a Tanner never fails to carry out a hit. Alonso Alvarado is a dead man."

Alexa looked thoughtful, and Tanner could see her relax.

"Yes, that's true, isn't it?"

"Absolutely."

"Don't forget to wake me when you come up."

"Count on it."

Alexa sent him a little wave and then disappeared. Tanner sat at the kitchen table, while going over Spenser's plan in his mind. Once again, he found it to be a sound strategy, and likely their only chance.

"A Tanner never fails," he said to himself, and knew it to be true.

9

THE BOOK OF TANNER

The following morning, in Oklahoma City, Ariana O'Grady left the hospital while wearing a diagonal bandage on her face. It ran from right to left and covered a cut that started at her upper lip and ended above her brow. The doctor told her that she just missed losing an eye, as Alexa's blade had scratched her left cornea.

Brick walked along beside Ariana as she was wheeled outside. Brick's neck was heavily bandaged on the left side, where Tanner had impaled him. After the nurse left them, Brick pointed toward the parking lot.

"I went and got the Lexus. Where do you want me to take you?"

Ariana just stood there looking lost. Instead of answering Brick, she asked a question of her own.

"What are the odds of us finding Tanner and the woman again?"

"Not good, but the word is that they're in Texas."

"He's headed for Mexico. He'll try to kill the man that wants him dead."

"Yeah, and he and the woman will die there."

Ariana looked around again. "I want to go home to Colorado. Will you take me, Brick?"

"Whatever you want, Ariana. If Tanner makes it out of Mexico somehow, I'll help you kill him."

"Thank you. Bring the car around, I just want to go home."

Brick went off to get the car and Ariana stood alone. As a young couple walked past her, she saw them both flinch as they got a look at her face.

If Tanner made it out of Mexico, she wouldn't go looking for him again, but if he ever set foot in Colorado, she vowed she would kill him. Still, the person she really wanted was Alexa. If she got her hands on her, she would slice her face to bloody ribbons.

∼

After his stint at guard duty the night before, Tanner didn't fall asleep until nearly six a.m.

When he woke, he was surprised to find that he had slept past noon, and then was pleased when he realized his ribs no longer hurt. After sitting up on the edge of the bed, he examined the wound to his calf and saw it was healing nicely.

He took a long shower, dressed, and made his way downstairs, where he found that he was just in time to join everyone for lunch.

Alexa kissed him in greeting, then asked him how he felt.

"I'm better. My ribs don't hurt, but I think I'll give myself another day before we travel."

"We'll need the time anyway," Spenser said. "And I'd like to get some target practice in after we eat lunch."

"Count me in on that," Tanner said.

Amy and Alexa had combined their culinary skills and made both lunch and dinner. The aroma of a baked ziti was in the air as everyone had a lunch of homemade chicken noodle soup and bacon, lettuce, and tomato sandwiches.

When Alexa teased the Horsemen about their nicknames, Amy asked them what their real names were.

"I know that Abrasion is Lionel and that Scar is Johnny, but what are your real names Bruise and Wound?"

"Eddie," Bruise said, and then he smiled, which displayed the gap in his teeth. The gap was the result of a kick from Alexa when they were on opposite sides in Oklahoma.

"And I'm Sean," said Wound, whose hair was the lightest of the four of them and would likely turn blond if he spent a lot of time in the sun. After answering, Wound looked over at Tanner. "What's your first name?"

"Tanner."

"Huh? Then what's your last name?"

"Tanner. I'm just Tanner."

∼

ONCE LUNCH WAS OVER, THE TIN HORSEMEN WENT OUT IN front of the house and played with a Frisbee.

As they were doing that, Amy started on the lunch dishes, while Tanner, Spenser, and Alexa were in the basement gun room, readying rifles for target practice.

"I took the book out of the safe last night, Cody," Spenser said.

Tanner smiled. "How did you know I would have something to add to it?"

"You always do, and except for Tanner Five, I think you have more entries than any of us."

"What is this book you're talking about?" Alexa asked, and Tanner explained.

"It's an old leather-bound book with blank pages toward the back, but at the front there are a handwritten list of tactics and strategies. The first Tanner started it, and we've all followed suit."

"Are you serious? How old is this book?"

Spenser was looking through a scope with his good eye, after determining that it was smudged, he cleaned it with a cloth.

"The first entry concerns events that took place about a hundred years ago, it's a long one, and it's autobiographical. After that, Tanner One wrote down different tactics and things, the clever ways he had fulfilled a contract. It was handed down to Tanner Two when he came along, and he followed suit, and after his autobiography, he lists his tactics. The book is a real goldmine of ingenious ways to kill and survive. Cody here has come up with a few of the best ones."

Alexa grinned. "Oh my God, I would love to read it."

"It's only for Tanners, Alexa," Spenser said, and then he added, "Of course, it would be Cody's call, since he's Tanner now."

Alexa held up a hand. "No, I don't want to see it; I like the idea that only a Tanner can read it, it's part of the myth and mystique."

Tanner and Spenser looked at each other and smiled. Alexa caught the exchange and stared at both of them.

"Did I say something funny?"

"No," Tanner said, "It's just that you sometimes act like a groupie around us."

She laughed. "I can't help it. I grew up listening to stories about the exploits of Tanner Five, and for me, meeting you two is like meeting royalty."

~

They moved outside with the rifles After setting up paper targets on several trees at the edge of the property, Tanner, Spenser, and Alexa began target practice.

Alexa was very good with a rifle, but she shook her head more than once in admiration of Tanner's skill at long distance shooting. She thought it remarkable when at one point he hit a target that was more than a mile away.

The Tin Horsemen had gathered to watch the exhibition. When Abrasion joined in with the sniper rifle that had belonged to the late strike team member, Hakeem, he found that he couldn't hit even the edge of a target, and the other Horsemen laughed at him.

Abrasion gave up after a dozen shots and headed for the house. Alexa felt bad for him and offered to give him a lesson.

"No thanks," he called back over his shoulder.

"Dude, bring back some sodas," Scar called to him.

~

Amy had been looking into the refrigerator. When she closed the door, she jumped, as she found Abrasion standing behind it.

"Oh Lionel, you scared me."

Abrasion sent her a stupid grin. "I just came inside to use the bathroom, and Scar asked me to get some soda."

Amy opened the fridge and grabbed a six-pack of cola. When she handed it to Abrasion, their fingers touched, and she saw him shiver.

"You're very pretty, Amy."

"Um, thank you, Lionel, but you know, I'm with Spenser. I'm also old enough to be your... older sister."

"I know," Abrasion said, as he continued to stare at her.

"Is there anything else you need, Lionel?"

"Huh?"

"Never mind, and why don't you take the soda outside."

"Okay, but hey, Amy."

"Yes?"

"If you and Spenser ever break up, you let me know."

"I'll do that."

Abrasion smiled as he left the kitchen whistling, and Amy let out a sigh.

10
BANG BANG

Alexa called her Papa Rodrigo in Mexico and heard both worry and wonder in his voice when she told him she was with Tanner. When she revealed that she was also with Spenser, Tanner Six, he asked to speak to him. Spenser and Rodrigo spent several minutes discussing Tanner Five, a man who had meant much to both of them.

The last thing Rodrigo said to Spenser, was to ask him to keep his daughter safe. Spenser told him that he would do just that, before handing the phone back to Alexa.

Alexa had grown less wary of the Tin Horsemen and it was decided that a night watch wasn't necessary. Instead, Spenser would set up motion detectors in strategic areas. If any of the Horsemen decided to roam about overnight, an alarm would alert Spenser.

As they soaked in a tub together, Alexa extended a long shapely leg and touched Tanner gently on the side with her toes.

"How are the ribs feeling?"

"They're good, but now my shoulder aches from all the shooting we did today."

"So does mine, and I was awed by your skill with a rifle. You never missed once."

"I've always been good with a rifle."

Alexa moved closer and kissed him, before laying back in his arms. "You're good at many things."

They grew quiet as they both enjoyed the warmth of the tub, as well as each other's company. Alexa had lit several candles and placed them near the tub, while music played softly from an old boom box she had discovered in a closet.

"I can't wait until you and Spenser meet my papa, and his companion, Emilio. The two of them raised me after my family died."

"I saw their pictures on your phone. The three of you looked very happy together."

"We were. Despite what I suffered when my family died, I had a great childhood thanks to Rodrigo. And although it wasn't a typical upbringing, I was glad he never sheltered me from life. He was a thief and proud of it, and he never apologized for it."

"He sounds wise, most people spend their lives pretending to be something they're not, instead of trying to be the best of what they really are."

Alexa turned in Tanner's arms and stared into his eyes. "You're a killer."

"Yes."

"So am I, but I don't think it's what I was meant to do."

"What were you meant to do?"

"I want to be a mother and raise a child, maybe more than one, and I want to forget that evil such as Alvarado exists in this world."

"It sounds like the quiet life."

"It will be," Alexa said.

Tanner kissed her, then she lay back in his arms again.

"Alexa, who taught you how to fight, was it Rodrigo?"

"Papa taught me the basics, but no, I had a judo instructor, and there was another man… from him I learned about guns."

"This man with the guns, he was a lover, wasn't he?"

Alexa turned her head until she could see Tanner's face. "How did you know that?"

"I heard something in your voice, and I can also tell that it was a serious relationship."

"It was, for me at least."

"He cheated on you?"

"Yes, and she was a friend."

"He was a fool to choose her over you."

"How can you say that? You don't even know her."

Tanner caressed Alexa's cheek. "I don't have to know her; I know you."

"What about you, Tanner? Do you have a woman somewhere that I should know about?"

"I was seeing a woman named Sophia, but she dumped me so that she could be with someone else. Alvarado killed her when he thought he was killing me, and so that's one more thing I owe the man."

"This Sophia, did you love her?"

"No, but we were friends."

"Have you ever been in love?"

Tanner released a deep sigh, before whispering, "Yes."

"And what happened to her?"

"She's married now."

"We're quite a pair you and I," Alexa said.

"That we are."

Alexa stood, stepped from the water, and grabbed a towel to dry herself.

When Tanner got out of the tub, Alexa looked him up and down, admiring his nakedness.

"You appear to be unarmed, sir."

Tanner removed the towel she had wrapped herself in and gazed at her body. The sight of her loveliness caused a reaction, one that did not go unnoticed by Alexa. She slowly licked her lips as she took in his changed condition, then spoke in a voice made husky with lust.

"You might be unarmed, but you're fully loaded."

"Bang bang," Tanner said, and they moved toward the bed.

11
WOUNDED HEART

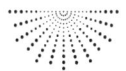

Tanner awoke the following morning to find that he had received the latest satellite images of Alvarado's compound. They were sent by Dan Matthews, who also requested that Tanner call him.

The Tin Horsemen had all behaved during the night and seemed boisterous over breakfast, as they debated the merits of a popular TV show that featured zombies. Their banter was often humorous, and even Tanner laughed at some of the things they said.

When Tanner called Dan Matthews, he did so in the presence of Alexa and Spenser and placed the call on speakerphone. They were down in the home's basement and standing around a pool table that was littered with satellite images of Alvarado's compound.

"You have news?" Tanner asked.

"Those satellite images are all the news you need, Tanner. There are hundreds of men surrounding that compound and the desert beyond it. As soon as you come within a mile of that place Alvarado will eat you alive."

"I'm aware of that, but since Alvarado won't leave the

compound, I have to go to him."

"Yes, but how will you do it? You must have a plan."

Tanner looked at Spenser and then Alexa. "What do you two think?"

"I think that having Conrad Burke on our side would be a big help," Spenser said.

"I agree," Alexa said. "And we need more information if our plan is to work."

"If I reveal our plan, would Burke be willing to help us carry it out?"

"Yes, Mr. Burke instructed me to give you every assistance I could. In exchange, you'll see that his brother-in-law emerges from that compound safely."

"All right then, our plan is to charge into Mexico and head straight for Alvarado while causing as much damage to the man's operation as we can. Then, once we get close to that desert fortress of his, we'll change tactics and enter the compound inside one of the trucks that deliver food."

"That will never work, every vehicle is searched and there are also dogs."

"We understand that, but we'll be well hidden, and our scents will be masked."

"That sounds risky, but I suppose it could work. How can Burke help you?"

"You're a giant corporation, and although you don't do business with Alvarado, I'm sure you must have connections with businesses in Mexico that do deal with the man. We need you to find out the name of the company where Alvarado gets his food shipments, along with the trucking firm that makes the deliveries. Once we have that information, we'll handle it from there."

"Fine, that shouldn't take long to ferret out. I'll send you an email when I have the information."

"Good, and give Burke my thanks."

"I will," Matthews said, then he hung up.

After putting his phone away, Tanner looked over at Spenser. "What do you think?"

"I think our plan is a go, but I do want to make a change."

"What change?" Alexa asked.

"The Horsemen, Johnny and his boys, I want to use them as backup for Amy. They're not much, but I think I'd feel better if she had them around. Martinez may expect them to be in Mexico anyway once they know we're there."

"You trust them enough to leave Amy alone with them?" Alexa asked.

"I do," Spenser said. "And they should be far from the action in any event."

Alexa smiled. "You may be right, and I think the one called Abrasion would die for Amy; he has quite a crush."

Spenser walked over to Tanner and looked him over. "How are you feeling, boy?"

"I'm good, and I doubt we'll see much action until we're in Mexico, so that gives me at least another day to heal. If everything is ready, I say we leave before noon tomorrow."

"I agree."

"I spoke with Dante again," Alexa said. "He told me that Sandoval will arrange to meet us in the Brownsville, Texas area, and then he'll help us cross the border without being spotted."

"Can this Sandoval be trusted?" Spenser said.

"Not at all," Alexa said. "But in this instance, our goals do align, so he has no need to double-cross us."

"Let's get Amy down here and go over the plan once more," Spenser said.

Alexa headed up the stairs. "I'll get her."

After Alexa disappeared up the stairs, Tanner told Spenser that he needed to apologize to him.

"Apologize for what, Cody?"

Tanner leaned back against the pool table as Spenser did the same and settled to his left.

"A few months back, while I was in New York City, an outfit called the Conglomerate put a price on my head. It was chump change compared to how much Alvarado is willing to pay to see me dead, but at one point, I faked my death and was thinking about starting over."

"Starting over?" Spenser said. "You mean give up the Tanner name?"

"Yeah, but I see now that if I had done that, it would have been like spitting in your face."

"I don't get you, Cody. How would that have been an insult to me?"

"You passed the Tanner name on to me when I was still very young. I don't think I fully appreciated just what an honor you gave me by doing that. Since I've met Alexa, I've come to remember how special it is to be a Tanner. I won't give up the name until I find someone to pass it on to myself."

Spenser smiled. "It's not a legacy that many would appreciate, being the best killer in the world. But I was always proud to be a Tanner, and Cody, you've only set the bar higher. I'm so proud of you, boy. Don't ever forget that."

"Thank you, but I just wanted you to know that I get it now, and that the name Tanner is more than a name. It's a statement."

Spenser quit leaning back on the pool table and placed a hand on Tanner's shoulder.

"This hit on Alvarado, the killing of a man who's as protected as he is. It will take you to a whole new level and leave no doubts that you, that Tanner, is the best assassin in the world."

"It's all I've ever wanted to be since the night Alvarado and his men killed my family. If I was then what I am now… I would have killed them all; I don't know how I would have done it, but I would have killed every last one of them."

Spenser stared into Tanner's eyes. On the night Tanner's family was massacred, Alvarado had arrived with over three dozen armed men who were experienced and merciless killers. Sixteen-years-old and untrained, Cody Parker managed to kill eight of those men while wounding others. The Cody Parker who stood before Spenser now was no longer a boy. He was highly trained, experienced, and had proven himself against those who were believed to be his better, such as the late German assassin, Hans Gruber.

If any man on the planet could not only survive, but triumph against such overwhelming odds, Spenser knew he was looking at him.

Spenser took his protégé by the shoulders. "You're the best, Cody, and don't ever doubt it."

Tanner grinned. "I had a great teacher."

～

When Alexa reached the kitchen, she had to stifle a chuckle, as she saw Abrasion handing Amy flowers. Alexa stood in the threshold and just watched the two of them, while remaining unnoticed.

"Where did you get these flowers, Lionel?"

"They're growing wild out back there and there's a few along the side of the house too."

"All right then, and thank you. I'll put them in a vase, and we can all enjoy them as a centerpiece for the dining room table."

"Okay, but I picked them just for you."

Amy sent Abrasion a patient smile. "We discussed this, Lionel, remember?"

Abrasion shook his head. "I wasn't hitting on you. I just saw the flowers and thought you should have them."

Amy smiled and gave him a peck on the cheek.

"That's fine, as long as you remember that I'm with Spenser and that you and I can only be friends."

"I get you, Amy," Abrasion said.

Alexa watched as he drifted out the back door, then she walked over to Amy with a grin on her face. "Someone has an admirer."

"He's a sweet boy, and I'm flattered."

"Still, can you imagine, thinking that you would be interested in him, after having been with a man like Spenser?"

"It's just a crush. Once he meets a girl his own age, he'll forget all about me."

"Spenser wants to see you in the basement; we need to go over the plan."

"All right," Amy said, and the two women headed for the basement steps, as they did so, they passed by an open window.

Outside that window, Abrasion stood with a handful of wildflowers he had just picked from the area alongside the house. He had overheard Amy and Alexa's conversation about him. After releasing the flowers, he stepped on them, as his face twisted in anger.

"I'm not a boy, Amy, I'm a man."

12

ONCE A SPY, ALWAYS A SPY

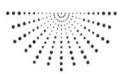

At the Alvarado compound in Mexico, Martinez looked at his phone with a face showing frustration, as his call to Scar went to voice mail once again.

"Call me!"

It had been two days since they last had news about Tanner, and Alvarado was becoming more agitated by the hour.

Once again, Martinez had been ordered to come to the drug lord's office. When he saw that Malena was also present for the meeting, he understood he had just about run out of time.

"Is there any news?" Alvarado asked.

Before answering, Martinez looked at Malena and saw that she wore a smug smile. When he turned back to Alvarado, he noticed the gun sitting on the desk, in easy reach of his right hand.

"Well, speak up," Alvarado said, and as Martinez opened his mouth to lie, his phone rang. When he saw the number displayed, he let out a sigh of relief.

"I need to take this call; It's about Tanner."

"Take it then," Alvarado said.

Martinez answered the call by saying the words, "Give me some good news," then he listened for several seconds, and as he listened, a smile formed on his lips.

"I'm with the client and his wife. I'm going to put you on speakerphone, and I want you to repeat what you just told me."

Martinez pushed a button, held up the phone, and a voice filled the room.

"I can confirm that Tanner is still with the woman and that a man is helping them as well. I also know how they're planning to enter the compound."

"How can you know their plans?" Malena Alvarado asked.

"Conrad Burke is helping Tanner. He wants Tanner to survive his encounter with you so that he can then utilize the man's skills. I know all this because I'm in the employ of Mr. Burke, although I do plan to retire after I'm paid handsomely for the information I have."

Those last words caused Martinez to grow angry. "You've already been paid by Hexalcorp, and paid a great deal."

"True," said the voice. "But that was when I was a simple corporate spy. I've been around long enough to know when I'm holding a winning hand. I want two million now and a million more when Tanner and his friends are dead. Do we have a deal?"

"I'll pay you what you ask," Alvarado said. "But I'll want proof that you can deliver what you say you can."

"I figured you would say that, and so I'll play a little recording. I made it when Tanner and the others revealed their plan."

A bit of background noise came through the phone, and then a voice was heard, Tanner's voice.

"You have news?"

"Those satellite images are all the news you need, Tanner. There are hundreds of men surrounding that compound and the desert beyond it; as soon as you come within a mile of that place Alvarado will eat you alive."

"I'm aware of that, but since Alvarado won't leave the compound, I have to go to him."

"Yes, but how will you do it. You must have a plan."

There was a short gap, and then Alvarado heard Tanner speak to his companions.

"What do you two think?"

A man spoke, and Alvarado recognized the voice. It belonged to the man who had crippled him.

"I think that having Conrad Burke on our side would be a big help."

"I agree," said a woman who spoke English with a Spanish accent. "And we need more information if our plan is to work."

"If I reveal our plan, would Burke be willing to help us carry it out?"

"Yes, Mr. Burke instructed me to give you every assistance I could—"

The recording ended abruptly.

"It was after that part of the conversation that Tanner revealed their plan to get inside the compound. Once two million dollars has been transferred into my account I'll play the rest of the recording."

Alvarado was sitting in his specially designed chair. He leaned forward to get closer to Martinez's phone.

"Who are you?"

"My name is Dan Matthews, Alvarado. I'm the man who can finally hand you Tanner."

"You will have your money," Alvarado said. "And then I will have my revenge."

13

OFF TO SLAY

The following morning, at sunrise, Tanner and Spenser went for a run, and the Tin Horsemen decided to tag along. What the boys failed to understand was that when a Tanner went for a run, he ran, and he ran full out.

After starting at a jog to warm-up, Tanner and Spenser turned on the speed and kept up a blistering pace. Bruise gave up somewhere along the second mile, While Scar and Wound faded halfway along the third. Abrasion gave his all to keep up with Spenser. It was a vain attempt to prove he was as good as Amy's one-eyed lover, but he soon fell far behind and came to a sudden halt early along the fourth mile, as a stitch in his side caused him agony.

Tanner and Spenser kept running along a route that circumnavigated the house. It was a simple two-mile-long dirt track. The fleet feet of the two Tanners kicked up a cloud of dust as they hurtled along.

When they came to the end of their fifth lap and tenth mile, first Spenser slowed, followed by Tanner. The two men jogged their final steps toward the home while breathing through their mouths, as sweat poured off them.

They had covered ten miles in a little more than an hour, and Tanner knew he was ready for Mexico.

Behind them, and cutting across the field, the Tin Horsemen came at a walking pace.

When Tanner and Spenser reached the porch, they found Amy and Alexa sitting in a pair of Adirondack chairs.

Amy's part in Spenser's plan was crucial, and part of it sat on a towing trailer attached to the rear of Scar's pickup truck. It looked like a large plastic-wrapped skid full of boxes, but inside its hollow center was a chamber large enough to hold three people.

It could be equipped with air tanks and when in use, it could also hold containers of ice to keep the interior cool.

The boxes beneath the plastic on the exterior were covered in Spanish with the names of major brands of Mexican food.

Amy had printed the logos on the boxes. They matched perfectly those of the real companies located in Mexico. The Tin Horsemen had helped her construct the cardboard Trojan horse, which could be entered from the top once the upper section was folded out of the way.

The entire thing was secured to an old wooden skid and looked like a million other pallets of goods. They would be shipping it to Mexico inside a crate, where it would be retrieved by Dante and waiting for them.

Tanner and Spenser looked at Alexa, and then at Amy.

"Well, what do you think?" Amy said, as she gestured toward her work.

Tanner gave Amy's creation a good look and followed it with a broad smile.

"It's perfect, Amy," Tanner said. "And once it's delivered to his compound, Alvarado won't know what hit him."

Spenser went to Amy, reached down, and pulled her from the chair by her hands.

"This plan will work. We leave for Mexico today."

∿

After breakfast, Alexa spoke with Dante, Damián Sandoval's man, and learned that Alvarado had stepped up his efforts to discover her identity.

"He has over a hundred people showing your picture around in Mexico City and the surrounding area," Dante said.

Alexa thought about Rodrigo and Emilio. Once Alvarado learned her identity, it wouldn't be long until he discovered her connection to them.

"How did you learn about this?"

"One of Alvarado's people showed the sketch of you to one of the people loyal to me. This has been going on for two days. If you have any connection to Mexico City, Alvarado will uncover it."

Alexa had several connections to the city, and once owned a jewelry store there. She thanked Dante for the tip, confirmed their plans to meet with Sandoval, and ended the call.

When she tried to reach Rodrigo, she was only able to leave a message on an answering machine warning him to take Emilio and leave their house.

"Call me as soon as you get this message, Papa. I love you."

∿

Alexa filled Tanner and Spenser in as they were outside the house and packing her van before leaving for

Mexico. After overhearing the conversation, Amy had a suggestion.

"Why don't I go with the boys and get your family to safety?"

Amy was talking about the Tin Horsemen when she said, "the boys", as she was flying to Mexico with them, while Tanner, Alexa, and Spenser headed for Brownsville, Texas, to meet with Damián Sandoval.

Scar and the other Horsemen stood by their pickup and listened to the conversation.

Alexa looked relieved by Amy's offer, but Spenser held up a hand in protest.

"That's too dangerous, Amy. What if Alvarado's men are there when you arrive? You'd be walking into a trap."

"I won't be stupid about it, Spenser. I'll only approach the house if Alexa's father answers my call, then we'll take them somewhere safe."

"It's still risky," Spenser said.

"Risky or not, it's what I want to do. You three will be in great danger every second you're in Mexico. Keeping Alexa's family safe is the least I can do, and I will have the boys backing me up."

"We're not boys," Abrasion said.

Amy sent him a smile. "It's just an expression, Lionel."

Alexa spoke to Spenser. "I understand your fear for Amy's safety, but it would give me peace of mind to know that someone was looking out for my family."

Spenser considered Alexa's words, then stared at Amy. "You be careful and call me as soon as you get to the rendezvous point. My phone will probably be off, so leave a message."

AMY AND THE HORSEMEN LEFT FIRST, AS THEY WERE taking a commercial flight into Mexico. Tanner, Alexa, and Spenser had a short drive to make to a local airfield, where they would board the private plane that belonged to one of Spenser's former clients.

The former client would fly them into Texas, then they would drive into Brownsville for their meeting with Sandoval.

Spenser and Amy shared a long kiss goodbye, as Abrasion stared at them with eyes full of envy. When the kiss ended, Amy opened the door to get in the rear seat of the pickup, but Spenser reached past her to offer Abrasion his hand.

Abrasion stared at Spenser's hand in surprise, but then shook it.

"Take care of Amy for me, all right?"

"Yeah," Abrasion said. "I'll make sure she stays safe."

"Good man," Spenser said. He then stood beside Tanner and Alexa, and waved goodbye.

When Alexa returned inside the home to finish packing, Tanner remained outside with Spenser.

"Hey Cody," Spenser said, as he watched the pickup carrying Amy grow smaller as it gained distance.

"What is it, Spenser?"

"I'm going to ask Amy to marry me when this is over."

Tanner laid a comforting hand on his mentor's shoulder. "She'll be fine, Spenser."

"I know she will, and she'll keep Alexa's father safe too."

Less than an hour later, they were ready to leave, and after checking the house before locking it up, Spenser joined Tanner and Alexa inside the van.

"Cody."

"Yeah?"

"Let's go show 'em how it's done, boy."

"Yes sir," Tanner said, and after placing the van in gear, they went off to slay.

14

YOU CAN ALMOST FEEL IT

The Alvarado compound was alive with activity, as Alvarado prepared to thwart Tanner's plans to invade his fortress.

He stood by the entrance as he balanced himself on his crutches, while watching as a work crew added even more fortification to the front gates.

Dan Matthews had betrayed Tanner and the others. He was two million dollars richer for the act, with the promise of a million more to follow once Tanner was dead.

After he played the rest of the recorded conversation he'd had with Tanner—while leaving out the section concerning Martinez' familial connection to Burke—Spenser's plan was revealed.

Alvarado had sent money to Matthews' offshore account, while supplying him false information to pass along to Tanner the next time he spoke with him.

When the trailer arrived with the hollow wrapped skid of goods that Amy had fashioned, Alvarado would be ready.

Specialized equipment was being gathered that would

detect heat signatures, along with another device that would pick up heartbeats.

Once in place, every large vehicle would be searched using the equipment. When Tanner, Spenser, and Alexa were detected, Alvarado planned to take all three of them alive, so that they could be tortured.

Earlier, he sat at his desk imagining the things he would inflict upon Spenser. Simply imagining it brought him so much pleasure that he nearly climaxed.

Tanner was a major problem, Alexa, an impudent bitch that needed to die, but Spenser, Spenser was special. The man had come into Alvarado's home and damn near killed him, while also giving Damián Sandoval the opportunity he needed to take over their former cartel and oust Alvarado from power.

Over the years, finding Spenser and paying him back for the agony he inflicted had nearly become a raison dêtre for Alvarado. Repaying Spenser in kind for the physical pain and mental anguish he had inflicted upon him was Alvarado's driving force.

He had regained power years ago, yet still felt unfulfilled because he had yet to achieve the retribution he so desired.

That would change, because Spenser would place himself within arm's reach, and once Alvarado had the man in his grasp, he would take the art of torture to new heights. Spenser's agony would last for months, even long after his mind had been destroyed.

∼

Alvarado had just lowered himself into a golf cart to be ferried back to the house by a guard, when he saw Martinez running toward him smiling. When Martinez reached him, he took a moment to catch his breath, then he relayed the good news.

"We got a nibble on that flyer with the sketch of the woman who is helping Tanner. A guy at a Pemex station in Mexico City says she used to buy gas there every week for a van. Unfortunately, she paid cash. But at least we now know that we're looking for her in the right area."

"Yes, and if she lived or worked in the city my people will find out who she is; it's just a matter of time."

"I've got a man at the gas station looking through old surveillance video, so there's also a chance we'll see her on film. If we can read her license plate, we can track her that way and learn her name."

"Excellent, at last things are going my way. Once we know who that bitch is, I'll send men to find her family."

"All right," Martinez said. "Although it seems anticlimactic now that we know Tanner's plan to infiltrate the compound."

"One can never have too much leverage, Martinez, remember that. The best way to make an enemy suffer is to kill their loved ones."

Alvarado held a hand out in front of him and rubbed his fingers together, as a look of bliss came over him.

"Oh, I can almost feel their blood."

15

WELCOME TO MEXICO

BOCA CHICA STATE PARK, BROWNSVILLE, TEXAS

Alexa drove their rented SUV off Highway 4 and onto Boca Chica beach, as Tanner and Spenser scanned their surroundings with a pair of binoculars. It was a weekday and post vacation season, so the beach crowd was sparse.

When they approached the north end of the beach across from South Padre Island, Spenser and Tanner lowered their binoculars and pointed out to Alexa the four men standing by a limo, which was parked near the shoreline.

"The man on the far right is Dante Cardoso," Alexa said.

"The other three look like cops," Tanner said. "And I'm a wanted fugitive in Mexico."

"They might be cops," Alexa said. "Damián Sandoval

owns many Federales, and they will do as he tells them to do."

Alexa brought the vehicle to a stop and Dante approached them with his arms held out from his side to show that he wasn't holding a weapon, although the bulge of a holster was clearly visible beneath the blue denim jacket he wore.

When Tanner stepped out of the van, Dante and the other men stared at him for long moments, and when Tanner gazed back at them, he saw a mixture of respect and caution in their eyes.

"Hello Anna… or should I call you Alexa?"

Alexa let out a gasp, and then asked a question.

"Are you telling me that Alvarado knows my name?"

"If he doesn't, he soon will, I just thought it was time the two of us stopped playing games. There must be trust if we're to continue to help each other, no?"

Dante moved closer and offered Tanner his hand. "You are Tanner, and if even a fraction of what I've heard about you is true, Alvarado will soon be having a very bad day."

Tanner shook the offered hand and then introduced Spenser as Tucker Coe.

Tucker Coe was the phony name that Spenser had used years ago, when he and Tanner had first met in Stark, Texas.

After the greetings were finished, Dante pointed at the men he had with him. "As you've probably guessed, those men are Federales; they'll be taking us across the border to meet Sandoval."

"He's agreed to help us?" Alexa said.

"He has, but he'll only offer information and materials, no troops."

"We're our own troops," Tanner said. "What we need are weapons and supplies. We're going to cut a path through Alvarado's organization on our way to him, to give him a taste of what to expect."

Dante laughed. "Just the three of you?"

"Just the three of us."

Dante studied Tanner, and the smile left his face.

"As requested, we retrieved the crate you had flown to Dallas. It's riding a drug transport plane to Mexico City. I'm going to guess that whatever is in that crate is part of your plan to breach the compound, but unless it's the world's smallest tank, I fear you will be unsuccessful."

"We'll see," Tanner said.

Dante smiled at Alexa. "You said that you would find Tanner and you did."

"Yes, I did, and together we will kill Alvarado."

Dante turned to walk back to the limo, as he did so, he gave instructions. "Follow behind the limousine and I'll take you to see Sandoval."

They did as instructed, and within minutes, they were entering Mexico.

PART II
THE EVE OF DESTRUCTION

16

MACHINATIONS

On the edge of the city of Matamoros, Mexico, Tanner, Alexa, and Spenser met with Damián Sandoval. The meeting took place in an alleyway between two storefronts, where several men with rifles overlooked the scene from the rooftops.

Damián Sandoval stepped out from the rear of a bulletproof limo and smiled at Alexa. "I see that you are someone who does what she says she'll do. That is a rare trait, particularly among your sex."

Alexa knew she should let Sandoval's sexist comment pass, but she couldn't help but respond to it.

"You believe that women are less honorable than men?"

Sandoval gave his head a small shake. "No, but they do possess far less fortitude. You however are an exception, and you continue to surprise me."

Sandoval then turned his gaze on Tanner. "I've learned the details of what you did to Alvarado's men in New York State, and your reputation is well earned, but do you truly believe that you'll be able to kill Alonso Alvarado?"

"Yes."

"Then you are either a fool or the best assassin who has ever lived."

Sandoval tossed his chin at Spenser. "This man, is he as good at killing as you are?"

"No," Tanner said. "He's better."

Damián Sandoval stepped closer to Spenser. "Why do you want to kill Alonso Alvarado?"

"I need to finish what I started."

"Meaning?"

"I'm the man who attacked him at his villa years ago and left him for dead. Up until about a week ago, I believed he was dead."

Sandoval broke into a wide grin and offered Spenser his hand. "I owe you a debt of gratitude. If not for your attack on that villa my rise to power might have been delayed for years."

Spenser took the offered hand and shook it. "It was my pleasure, and soon we'll finish the job. But tell me, just how did that bastard make it out of the house? The place was an inferno and he couldn't sit up, much less walk."

Sandoval relayed to them the story of how Carlos Ayala saved Alvarado, and Spenser grew angrier at himself for having failed.

"Dante," Sandoval said, and Dante walked over to stand beside his boss.

"Yes sir?"

"Give these three what they need. Sadly, they won't succeed, but they will cause Alonso grief before they die; that is worth much to me."

"We will kill Alvarado," Alexa said. "And if you're as smart as they claim you are, you'll be ready to take over that compound of his when we do."

Sandoval stepped closer to Alexa, and being a small man, he stood an inch shorter than she did.

"You are a beautiful woman and you have the heart of a warrior. Your companions are extremely capable men, and while this plan of yours has merits, you will still be vastly outnumbered."

Alexa stared at Sandoval with defiance. "We will not fail."

Sandoval turned from her, while shaking his head sadly. "Such a sad waste of a fine woman."

Afterwards, he climbed back inside the limo and disappeared behind tinted glass.

Dante walked over to a door at the side of the building on their left and asked that Tanner, Alexa, and Spenser follow him inside, as the limo roared to life.

The old building was a long narrow warehouse that held only empty shelves. Overhead lights dangled from the ceiling, and they walked from one circle of light into another, as they moved across a concrete floor that here and there showed stains and displayed cracks.

Dante soon entered a glass-enclosed office, where he stepped behind a desk. When Tanner and his companions stood before him, Dante pointed at a blank pad that had a pen laying on it.

"Write down any supplies you need, but in Spanish. I can speak English, but I can't read or write it for shit."

"The thing that would help us most is transportation," Tanner said.

Dante nodded. "We'll fly you to Mexico City and give you a place to stay."

Spenser rubbed a hand over his beard. "A plane is risky, but it would speed up our timetable."

"We'll be using Sandoval's private jet. Trust me, it's safe, and I'll be flying with you."

"Fine," Tanner said. "And it'll likely be the least risk we'll be facing."

Alexa grabbed the pen and looked at Tanner. He named a few items, mostly weapons, and then added one that made Dante smile, while also causing Alexa to give Tanner a quizzical look. Tanner had told her to get a dress, and the sexier the better.

"It will be used as a weapon," he said.

Alexa gave him a doubtful, yet knowing look, and Spenser laughed at her expression.

Before leaving the warehouse, they solidified their plans concerning the phony pallet of goods that they hoped to smuggle inside the compound. Dante told them he would handle getting it onto the truck that made the deliveries.

"What about the driver?" Alexa asked. "Will he cooperate?"

"He will once we kidnap his wife," Dante said.

"Couldn't you just bribe him?" Alexa asked.

"If we used only greed he might betray us, but he is a young man who recently married. He will do anything to protect his bride. Fear usually works better than greed."

"Do not harm her in any way," Alexa said. "Killing and using the relatives of an enemy is Alvarado's way, not ours."

Dante smiled at her. "Don't worry, the men I'll be using are professionals. But understand something, if you fail to kill Alvarado, he will kill the driver and his wife for helping you."

"He won't get the opportunity," Tanner said.

Dante smiled at the three of them. "Ah, if I had a touch more madness in me, I would join you, but as I've grown older, I've grown wiser. Still, I'm betting that you'll be successful."

"We'll need a place to stay tonight once we reach

Mexico City," Spenser said. "And tomorrow we start handing grief to Alvarado."

There was a brown envelope on the desk. Dante picked it up and handed it to Spenser.

"That's a partial list of Alvarado's drug couriers in the Mexico City area. But I warn you, do not attempt to kill any of these men near one of the meth labs, their security is tight."

Spenser took the envelope but gestured toward Alexa. "She has her own list of targets."

Dante grinned. "That's right; you were busy killing Alvarado's people even before you breached the compound."

"Yes, and with the help I have now, what I did before will be nothing in comparison."

When they left the warehouse, Tanner took note that the snipers were gone from the rooftops. He assumed they were a part of Sandoval's private guard.

Dante stared at the three of them in turn, before locking eyes with Spenser. "The last time you attacked Alvarado, it gave Sandoval the opportunity he needed to rise to power."

"Yes, and?" Spenser said.

Dante looked around to make sure that none of the other men were in hearing range, then spoke again.

"My boss believes you will fail. And yet, it occurs to me that if you were to succeed, someone would have to step in to fill the power vacuum left behind."

Tanner, Alexa, and Spenser all traded looks, then turned their attention back to Dante.

"For a man to make such a bold move," Tanner said. "He would still need help controlling Alvarado's troops, but yes, it will be a once in a lifetime opportunity."

Dante took out a phone, fiddled with it, and held it up.

On the screen was a close-up photo of a young man with curly brown hair, and there was a tattoo of a cross on the man's neck.

Dante looked at Alexa. "You do remember Joaquin, yes?"

"Of course."

"When the trouble begins, he will help you, and if you are successful, he will signal me. Do you understand?"

"Understood," Tanner said. "But you'll need your own men if you're going to take over that compound."

Dante smiled. "I have them. They're the men from the villages surrounding the compound. Alvarado crossed the line when he killed those prostitutes. They were worthless whores to him, but to the men from the villages, they were their daughters and sisters. I also have the police around the area of the compound in my pocket, although they weren't cheap."

Tanner looked at Dante with a new appreciation.

"It would seem that Sandoval isn't the only one who knows when to take advantage of a situation."

Dante gave a single nod. "In this world, you either rule or serve, and I've grown tired of serving."

"You'll get that signal," Tanner said, and Dante laughed with pleasure.

17
HURRY UP AND WAIT

Amy arrived in Mexico with the Tin Horsemen and was unable to contact Rodrigo by phone.

After leaving Spenser's home, they had driven to Yellowstone Regional Airport and made sure that the crate they towed was loaded onto the cargo plane.

That went smoothly, but then their own flight was cancelled due to a mechanical problem, and Amy and the Tin Horsemen spent several boring hours waiting to board another plane.

They finally arrived in Dallas, only to learn that their connecting flight to Mexico City would also be delayed. By the time they landed in Mexico and cleared customs, it was nearly midnight.

Amy had tried all day to get in touch with Rodrigo with no success. When she spoke to Alexa from the airport in Mexico City, she learned that Alexa had made calls and discovered that Rodrigo and Emilio had visited Emilio's sister in Durango, after learning that she had become ill.

The illness turned out to be just a stomach flu, and Rodrigo and Emilio were on their way back home.

"It's a long drive and Papa will stay somewhere overnight," Alexa had told her. "He carries his cell phone when he travels, but knowing Papa, he probably forgot to turn it on."

Amy told Alexa not to worry, and that she and the Horsemen would go to the house and wait for them to come home, and then take them to safety.

Spenser voiced his concern for the delay, reminding her that Alvarado would eventually send men to the home, But Amy told him she would do all she could to help Alexa, and not to worry.

"I love you, Amy," Spenser told her.

"I love you too, Spenser, and I'll gather up Alexa's family and meet you at the rendezvous point you told us about, don't worry."

~

AFTER RENTING A LARGE SUV WITH SATELLITE navigation, Amy input the address for Rodrigo's home, and she and the Tin Horsemen began the two-hour drive to the house in San Juan Del Rio.

While the other three horsemen slept in the back seat, Abrasion sat up front with Amy.

"You've been quiet today, Lionel. Is anything wrong?"

"No Amy, I'm good."

"I can't thank you and the others enough for accompanying me on this trip. I think I would be very nervous if I was alone, and I'm so scared for Spenser. It's like he'll be walking into the lion's den."

Abrasion said nothing. Amy took her eyes from the dark road and glanced at him again.

"Are you sure you're okay?"

"I'm fine, but maybe I should try to catch some sleep too. Wake me if you need me to drive."

After saying that, Abrasion crossed his arms and leaned over toward the door with his face turned away from her.

Amy gave him another glance, then she placed her gaze back on the road and chewed up the miles that separated them from Rodrigo.

Beside her, Abrasion pretended to sleep.

∽

THEY ARRIVED IN SAN JUAN DEL RIO AND DROVE TO THE house, just in case Rodrigo had driven straight home. There was no vehicle in the driveway and the home was dark, so Amy drove back to the highway where they checked into a motel.

After grabbing only a few hours of sleep, they were back at the home belonging to Rodrigo Lucia, Alexa's father. The house sat at the top of a slight hill, and there was a line of decorative ash trees to the left of it, while on the right, the street curved and continued toward Federal Highway 120, where it ended in a cul-de-sac of new homes.

Amy drove up the hill and pulled to the side of the road that was bordered by trees, while staying a few dozen yards from the home.

Alexa had described Rodrigo's vehicle, and said that it was a red Chevy Tornado, which was a small pickup truck. It was nowhere in sight.

"It looks like they're still not back yet," Bruise said, then he took a bite out of a breakfast sandwich they had grabbed on the way.

Scar opened his door and stretched. "I'll go check out the house and make sure everything looks normal."

The other Horsemen joined him, and Amy watched with a growing sense of apprehension as the boys walked around the well-maintained home. When they began walking back toward the vehicle, Scar sent Amy an "Okay" signal.

"Does everything look normal?" Amy asked, as the boys climbed back in the SUV.

"Yes," Abrasion said. "So, I guess we wait?"

"We wait," Amy said, as she looked around nervously. "And I certainly hope they return soon."

18

MIDNIGHT RENDEZVOUS

Roberto Muñoz liked his job on most days, but lately, it was a pain in the ass.

Roberto was a collector for the Alvarado cartel. He spent his work life going from one small business to another in Mexico City and picking up envelopes of cash. The money paid for protection, and although Roberto occasionally had to teach a late payer a lesson, the job was an easy gig.

Over the three years he'd had the job, only once did someone attempt to rob him, and they were a couple of young punks. Roberto shot one of the boys in the arm when the kid hesitated to pull the trigger on the shotgun he held. The pair got away but were stupid enough to seek medical attention at a nearby hospital.

For stopping the robbery, Roberto got a ten-grand bonus from Alvarado, while the two that attempted the robbery were sent home. They were sent home in packages, a piece at a time. As far as Roberto knew, no one had tried to rob any of Alvarado's people since then.

Roberto entered a shop that sold cigars and nodded in

greeting at the owner. The man nodded in return and took an envelope from the cash register, which he then handed to Roberto.

As he was about to leave the shop, Roberto remembered, let out a sigh, and showed the man the drawing of Alexa. He had been showing the drawing around for three days and hated doing it, despite the reward that would be his if he somehow found her.

During normal times, Roberto could finish his collections by noon, but it took time to show the picture and ask questions, and he knew he'd be lucky to make it back home by two.

The store owner shook his head, and Roberto told the man to hang up the flyer where people could see it. If anyone recognized the woman, they were to call the number at the bottom of the paper.

Before leaving the store, Roberto slipped the envelope of protection money into the satchel he carried, then took out another flyer to show the owner of the next business, which was across the street.

The woman that managed the store gave him the same dirty look she always gave him as she handed over her envelope. She was an employee, not the owner of the business, and Roberto wondered why she took things so seriously.

On the other hand, the woman's daughter always smiled at him. She did it once again, from where she was setting up a holiday display. The girl was cute, with long legs and a nice rack, but she was only nineteen or so. At thirty-nine, Roberto knew he would feel sleazy if he slept with her, seeing as how he had a daughter nearly her age.

Once again, he went through the routine with the flyer, but was shocked when the girl said that she knew who it was.

"You know this woman?"

The girl had walked over and moved behind the counter. "That's the lady that owned the jewelry store in the mall. The store is gone now, but look, I bought these earrings there."

Roberto looked at the tiny diamond stud earrings as the girl leaned across the counter, then his gaze drifted down to a view of the girl's cleavage. When he raised his eyes, she was smiling at him.

"Tell me which mall, and also the location of the store."

The girl reached under the counter and grabbed a pad and pen. "I'll write it down for you."

She did so, and when Roberto returned to his car, he noticed that she had written something in small letters beneath the name of the mall.

PICK ME UP IN FRONT OF THE STORE AT MIDNIGHT.

Next to that, she had drawn a heart.

Roberto laughed as he took out his phone to report what he'd learned, and yes, he was back at the store at midnight.

∼

Minutes later, at the compound, Alvarado told Martinez what Roberto had uncovered.

"One of my people found someone who says she knows the woman. She says that the woman helping Tanner once owned a jewelry store inside a Mexico City Mall."

"That's great; would you like me to send people to the mall?"

Alvarado smiled a wolf's grin. "No, I will send my

people. Once they make contact with the management there, it won't be long until we have a name. When that's known, we will find those she loves and use them against her."

Martinez grimaced as he thought about Alvarado getting his hands on his loved ones, such as his daughter, who lived with his ex-wife.

He had been holding his breath earlier when Dan Matthews made his deal with Alvarado, fearing that the man would reveal his ties to Conrad Burke, who was helping Tanner. Luckily, Matthews had failed to disclose that relationship.

Tanner couldn't make his move on the compound soon enough to suit Martinez, because once the man and his friends were captured, he would be free to leave, and there was a point there when he thought he might never make it out alive. Thank God, Alvarado was finally in a good mood.

"Martinez."

"Yes sir?"

"The next delivery truck is due Friday at noon. I want it kept outside the gates until Tanner and his friends are in chains."

"I assumed as much, and there will be dozens of men surrounding that truck when it's opened."

Alvarado looked alarmed. "Remember, I want them alive."

"Yes sir, the men are clear on that. The team opening the truck will be armed with only teargas and Tasers."

Alvarado sighed. "How I wish my son Juan had lived to see this day. He always said that I would find the man who crippled me, and now that day is finally here."

Martinez folded his hands in front of him. "I'm sure your son is looking down on you."

"What?"

"Your son, I 'm sure he's in heaven and looking down on you."

Alvarado stared at Martinez and searched his face. Had he detected even a trace of sarcasm or derision, he would have had him killed.

"Leave me."

After seeing the look in Alvarado's eyes, Martinez scurried from the office without uttering another word.

19
CHOP CHOP!

El Bar Del Primo in Mexico City was a private club for several of Alvarado's senior narcos, who at night would bring their girlfriends to hear the live local bands that played there.

In the afternoon, over lunch, they would often talk business. Four of them were gathered together at a back table while they waited for two more of their friends to show.

When a silver Maserati pulled up in front and two men stepped out of it, the big man guarding the front door unlocked it and placed his hand on the doorknob. That was when two booming shots echoed down the avenue and the men from the Maserati fell to the ground, each with gaping exit wounds where their faces had been.

"Out the back door!" shouted one of the men in the booth, and the four men raced down a hallway. When the first man reached the rear door and unlocked it, he went out slowly and with his gun arm leading the way.

There was a blur of movement, a flash of steel, and both the arm and the gun fell to the ground.

As the man who'd lost his arm gaped at his spurting stump in wonder, his companions turned around to head back into the club. That's when the big man who'd been guarding the front door plowed into them while in a blind panic.

All five men stumbled outside after the collision. Three had fallen, including the man who'd lost his arm. When he reached out to grab the severed limb with his other hand, he yelped in surprise, as a second, and then a third arm fell near him. He lost sight of all three limbs when a spray of blood filled his eyes.

Within seconds, the five men were lying on the ground, bleeding profusely from vicious wounds, while moaning. Their attacker, Alexa, looked down upon them with eyes devoid of mercy, and again she went to work with the twin swords she wielded.

With five efficient strikes, she put the men out of their misery, then removed a pair of blood-spattered goggles.

Spenser walked over and stared at her grim handiwork. "You didn't leave me anything to do. And I've never seen anyone handle swords so well, not even Cody."

Alexa dropped the swords. After taking off a pair of latex gloves, she lowered the hood on the bloody plastic coveralls she wore.

She had unzipped the coveralls and was stepping out of them when they heard an engine come from the alleyway entrance at the side of the club.

Spenser had raised his rifle, but he lowered it when the silver Maserati appeared with Tanner behind the wheel.

"Get in!" Tanner said, as he took in Alexa's handiwork.

The alley's rear ran the length of the block. Tanner took it to the other end and drove them from the scene while weaving around dumpsters and delivery vans. Inside the car, Alexa removed a travel-size package of moist towelettes and began wiping the blood of Alvarado's men from her face.

~

In San Juan Del Rio, Amy had to stop herself from biting her nails. She had developed the bad habit when she worked in Hollywood and had been the lead makeup person on several films. One had been a low-budget horror movie where people were turning into human frogs.

The film had been a disaster, but she had won praise for her skill with makeup and had moved on to bigger productions.

She didn't miss those days. They were full of stress, and while working with Spenser was ripe with tension at times, she never felt nervous as she did now.

But then again, when she worked with Spenser to help one of his clients, she was with Spenser, and whenever she was near Spenser, she always felt safe.

The Tin Horsemen had grown bored with waiting inside the vehicle. Scar had suggested that they walk around the area and keep watch.

Amy agreed with the idea, and when she returned from a bathroom break at a nearby coffee shop, the boys split up and walked the neighborhood to see if there was anyone around who looked, "thuggy" as Scar had put it.

Amy thought that Abrasion might use the opportunity to be alone with her, but no, he wandered off with the others. That was good, as edgy as she was, she didn't need a lovesick boy to fend off.

Amy took out her phone and gazed at one of the photos of Rodrigo and Emilio that Alexa had given her. Amy spoke to it, as if the men in the picture could hear her.

"C'mon, return home already; it's not safe to stay here."

A car came around the corner. When Amy saw that it was red, she thought it was Rodrigo returning, but no, the car drove past her and headed down the road toward the cul-de-sac.

And without even realizing it, Amy began to nibble on a fingernail again.

20

TANNER?

Two of Alvarado's enforcers were sent to the mall to ferret out Alexa's identity. The men were a pair of professional thugs, and their size and height intimidated most people.

The manager of the mall was no exception. He helped the men by searching through the store's records, while his fingers trembled on the keyboard of his computer. When they left the mall, the men had Alexa's name and address.

~

Alvarado wore a wide smile when he learned that his men had uncovered Alexa's name. He called his wife and asked her to come to his office. When she entered, he spoke before she had even closed the door.

"Alexa Lucia, that is the name of the woman who killed your brother."

Malena took a seat in front of the desk. "Alexa Lucia? I do not know that name, do you?"

"No, but we will discover the reason for her attack on the compound once we have her."

"She's mine, Alonso. You do whatever you want to Tanner and that other man, but the bitch is mine. I will make her pay for killing my brother."

"I agree, but you must keep your anger in check once she's here, otherwise she'll die too quick a death."

"Oh, she will suffer, trust me."

Alvarado's phone rang, and this time it was bad news, as he learned about the slaughter inflicted on his men by Tanner and Alexa.

When the call ended, he looked over at Malena.

"Tanner and his companions have killed several of my best men in Mexico City."

Malena looked alarmed. "What does that mean? Have they abandoned their plan to stowaway aboard the delivery truck?"

"No, those bastards are coming here. This attack is a diversion, and there will likely be more of them. Tanner is hoping I'll send some of the men guarding the compound into the city to search for him. But if I did that, he would have fewer men to face when he gets here."

Malena darkened with rage. "Good Lord, how I so hate that man, and I still hold him partly responsible for Juan's death."

"As do I. Let the bastard do as he wishes, after the delivery truck arrives tomorrow, we will have him before us on his knees."

Malena reached into a pocket on her dress and withdrew a blade, which she unfolded. The sharp edge of the weapon gleamed in the light coming through the windows.

"Alexa, the bitch who killed my brother, I cannot wait to have her at my mercy."

"Remember, my love, do not kill her quickly."

Malena smiled wickedly. "How many men are here, Alonso?"

"Nearly three-hundred outside the walls, and another dozen or so inside them, why?"

"The bitch, Alexa, I will stake her to the ground and let all the men have a turn with her, and after that humiliation is done, then she'll be mine to play with. I promise you, her end will not come swiftly."

Alvarado laughed, and Malena joined in, as they both reveled in what they believed was to come.

∿

In Mexico City, Hector Ramos put away his phone. He was the one who had informed Alvarado about the seven men who were murdered at the private club.

Hector was in his car and headed for a meeting. He and three others met twice a week for lunch at the home of one of the men, to discuss any problems that were going on with the distribution of product, as well as the growing threat posed by Damián Sandoval.

Alonso Alvarado had become obsessed with the trouble in New York City and his hunt for the man called Tanner. Meanwhile, Sandoval had been slowly encroaching on their territory.

It would seem that Alvarado was right to be concerned about Tanner, but Hector was secretly happy about the slayings. One of the men killed at the private club had been his rival within the cartel and had recently been chosen to hold a coveted position. Now that the man was gone, Hector would be tapped to take his place. That move upward would triple the amount of money he made. It would also mean more free time, something Hector desperately wanted so that he could be with his mistress more often.

He pulled into the driveway of his friend's home and could tell by the cars parked there that he was the last to arrive. Hector grinned, once he was moved up and running an entire district, he would hire a driver, and after a few more years had passed, he was certain he would be running the entire city.

Hector walked around and knocked on the back door as he always did, but his mind was in the future and pondering the glories and prestige that were to come.

As the door opened, Hector smiled in greeting, but the grin faded as he took in the bloody corpses of his friends, which were sprawled on the floor around a table.

The man who had opened the door was staring at him with the most intense gaze he had ever seen, and Hector had time to whisper one last word before he died.

"Tanner?"

21

TIME IS RUNNING OUT

The two thugs who had uncovered Alexa's name and address went to her apartment and discovered that she had moved out months earlier. One of them made a call, and several Federales owned by Alvarado came to the area to interview neighbors, while hoping to learn where Alexa had moved to after she had left her apartment.

The truth was that she had been living out of her van and a succession of motels, while she spent months gathering intel on the cartel and killing the men who worked for it.

Other Federales were searching her background, but that would take time and could involve bribes and threats.

When a neighbor suggested that another neighbor, a young woman named Sylvia, had been a friend of Alexa's when she lived in the apartment building, the Federales made talking to Sylvia their next priority.

They broke into Sylvia's apartment when they received no answer, and later learned that the woman was at her job in Churubusco, which was a thirty-minute drive.

The Federales got back in their vehicle and drove to

Churubusco to ask Sylvia what she knew about Alexa. Following right behind them were the two thugs Alvarado had tasked with finding Alexa's family. If Sylvia refused to talk to the Federales, she would not refuse to speak to them.

Great pain tended to loosen stuck tongues.

~

Amy nearly leapt out of her skin when her phone rang. She was still in her car and staring at Rodrigo's home, but Alexa's father and his companion had yet to come home from their trip.

The Tin Horsemen had returned to the car and were waiting with Amy. Scar and Bruise had walked to a restaurant on the highway and returned with lunch, but Amy had barely eaten, as her nervousness had made her lose all appetite.

"Hello?"

"It's me, honey; please tell me you have Rodrigo and Emilio?"

"No, Spenser, we're still waiting."

"Leave there, Amy. You've done all you can do, but Dante just called and told us that Alvarado knows Alexa's name, and knowing that, it won't be long until he finds out where Rodrigo lives."

"Oh God, but Spenser, I can't leave, Rodrigo must be warned."

"Alexa has left him numerous messages on his cell phone and the landline. Hopefully, he'll check his messages as soon as he walks in the door."

"Hopefully?"

"Yes, but in either event, you and the boys have to leave there, or you may be harmed."

"Are you at least close to us?"

"No, we're still in Mexico City."

Amy was silent for a moment. After taking a deep breath, she spoke. "I'm staying. I promised Alexa that I would get her father to safety and that's just what I'm going to do."

"Amy, this is no time to be stubborn. Baby, we're talking about your life here."

"I understand that, Spenser, and I won't change my mind. Tell Alexa that I will see her father to safety."

Amy heard Spenser curse beneath his breath, and it was followed by a sigh. "You are one stubborn woman, do you know that?"

Amy grinned. "I do, and we'll all see you at the rendezvous point later, I promise."

"I love you, Amy."

"I love you too, Spenser," Amy said, and sitting beside her, Abrasion balled his hands into fists.

∼

AFTER SPENSER ENDED THE CALL, HE SAW THAT ALEXA WAS looking at him. He, Tanner, and Alexa were preparing to cause Alvarado more grief, as they made plans in the rear parking lot of a convenience store in Mexico City.

"Amy is staying?"

"Yes, and it worries me."

"I'm concerned as well, but Papa should arrive home soon."

"We could head there now if you'd like to, Spenser?" Tanner said.

Spenser blew out a great sigh. "I would go there in a heartbeat if she was close, but it's two hours away, and Alexa's right, her father should be home soon. Let's just keep going here and I'll stay in touch with Amy by phone."

Alexa touched Spenser on the arm. "If it makes you feel any better, although I'm concerned, I'm not worried, and I feel that they will be all right."

Spenser smiled. "If you're not worried then I guess I shouldn't be either, so let's get back to work."

~

SYLVIA VENTA WAS SEATED INSIDE HER CUBICLE AT THE insurance company she worked at and was looking up at the two stone-faced Federales.

Sylvia had dyed red hair and had been eating lunch at her desk when the men appeared. She wiped her hands on a napkin and answered their questions.

"Yes, I know Alexa Lucia. She was a neighbor."

"We were told you were friends. Do you know where she's moved to?"

"No, and we were more like friendly than actual friends. But Alexa was friends with the woman who owned the gym we worked out at."

"What's the name of this gym?" the man asked, and then they were off to find another link in the chain that would lead them to Rodrigo's doorstep.

~

AMY AND THE BOYS WERE STANDING OUTSIDE THEIR RENTED SUV as she filled them in on the growing threat they faced.

"It's just a matter of time until some of Alvarado's men come here, so I want you guys to take the car and head to the rendezvous point."

Amy had handed Scar the keys. He stared at them as they sat in the palm of his hand.

"What? You want us to just leave you?"

"When Rodrigo shows, I'll ride with him and Emilio, but it's too dangerous for you to stay here."

Bruise looked torn. He hated any kind of pain and was smart enough to fear Alvarado, but he had enough heart not to leave an unarmed woman to fend for herself.

"Yo, Scar, we ain't leaving, are we?"

"No, we're not," Abrasion said. "I mean you guys do what you want, but I'm not leaving Amy here alone."

Amy grabbed his arm. "I want you all to go, Lionel. I wouldn't be able to forgive myself if any of you boys got hurt."

Abrasion freed his arm from her grip. "We're not boys, and I know I'm not as big and tough as Spenser, but I'm not a coward either. I'm staying."

Scar handed Amy back the keys. "We'll all stay, but we'll keep watch too. If we see anybody that doesn't look cool, we'll call you and give you the heads up."

Amy felt relieved and anxious at the same time, but she sent the boys a smile. "Thank you, guys."

Scar draped his arms over the shoulders of Bruise and Wound. "We're the Tin Horsemen; danger is our business."

Bruise and Wound agreed with Scar, but Abrasion said nothing. He was still angry that Amy had called him a boy again.

"Lionel," Amy said.

"Yeah?"

"Are you all right?"

"I'm fine, Amy," Abrasion said, but he wasn't. He had a broken heart.

22

BEAUTY TO DIE FOR

While riding in the rear of his stretch limo, Enrique De Jesús, had just learned about the second attack in the city, as four more narcos were found shot dead inside a home.

The murders had been called in by an anonymous tipster, but Enrique had no doubt that Tanner was behind the slayings.

Enrique De Jesús had been given the job of managing Mexico City after Rico Nazario was chosen to run New York City. The last thing Enrique needed was a nightmare like Tanner screwing things up.

His call to Alonso Alvarado had not gone as he expected. He had assumed that the man would send him help to deal with Tanner. But no, Alvarado seemed content to let the American do as he pleased.

Why not? Enrique thought. *Hell, if I was sitting inside an impenetrable fortress with an army to protect me, I wouldn't care what happened here either.*

It then occurred to Enrique that Tanner being in Mexico City could be a huge opportunity if he were to kill the man. If he could hand Tanner's corpse to Alvarado there would be nothing that the drug lord wouldn't give him. He would also leapfrog ahead of Rico Nazario as being the next in line to rule, since Rico had failed to kill Tanner when he had the chance.

Enrique's ruminations on the matter ended as he realized that his two bodyguards, who were seated across from him, were staring out the side window and grinning lasciviously.

It was a woman, and she was a hell of a woman. She was riding beside the limo in a jeep that had its doors and top removed.

The short red dress she wore exposed her long legs, as the wind pushed the hem of the dress even higher, while whipping her dark hair about in the breeze. Up top, was revealed a generous portion of her breasts, which jiggled with every bump in the road. Enrique found it impossible to take his eyes off her.

Enrique's bodyguards were practically drooling, and when the woman turned her head to look toward them, Enrique felt as if she were staring directly at him. But that wasn't possible because the windows were heavily tinted.

"Oh shit," one of the bodyguards said. "If that dress were any smaller she'd be naked."

Enrique didn't need the dress to grow smaller; he was already imagining the woman naked.

She was matching the limo's speed and continuing to stare at them, then, she smiled and winked.

"The bitch sees the limo and smells money," the second bodyguard said. "I bet she'd let you do anything you want to her, Mr. De Jesús."

Enrique smiled, then he reached for the button to roll the window down, a window made of bullet-resistant glass. The first bodyguard held up a hand in warning.

"Mr. De Jesús, maybe that's not a good idea, sir."

Enrique laughed at the man. "You worry too much, Sebastian, and she's too good to pass up. Besides, where the hell would she hide a gun in that dress?"

The window lowered, and Enrique smiled at the woman. Enrique was over forty, but he had stayed trim, was possessed of a dazzling smile, and wore enough bling to let any woman know he had serious money.

The woman smiled back at him, then she pointed up at the roof of a three-story apartment building.

The building was behind the sound barrier and nearly half a mile away, but Enrique could see that something up there was reflecting the sun. When he looked back at the woman, he saw that she had decreased her speed dramatically, while her car's turn signal indicated that she intended to take the next exit.

Enrique was about to tell the driver to follow her, but a high caliber rifle round put a hole in his chest the size of a baseball, and he died without ever knowing it.

The bodyguards both fumbled at the window controls, but two more shots ended their efforts, and the limo moved smoothly down the highway.

Up front, its driver sang along to a tune on the radio, oblivious to the fact that he was suddenly in control of a hearse.

~

Tanner was waiting for Alexa near the off-ramp. After she abandoned the stolen jeep, she walked over in a pair of six-inch heels and climbed into the car Tanner was driving.

"Spenser called; he made the shots," Tanner said.

"I'm surprised you didn't do it. I think you're a better shot than he is."

"I wanted to be close to you in case there was trouble."

"That's sweet, but all I had to do was wear this dress, and I feel like such a slut in it."

"Hold on to that dress, we may need it again."

"Really? You think this trick will work twice?"

"No, but you can wear it when we're alone."

Alexa laughed. "I'll do that, and what will you be wearing?"

Tanner ran a hand along her naked thigh.

"I'll be wearing a smile."

23
TRUCKIN'

Alvarado was growing impatient again, as the search for Alexa's loved ones seem to be taking too long. When he asked one of his sources why they couldn't trace her family by searching computer records, he learned that it was suspected her name might be an alias.

No one her approximate age with the name Alexa Lucia was listed with CURP, which was an acronym for Clave Única de Registro de Población. CURP was the agency that issued citizen ID numbers.

Alvarado told the man to find a source inside the Federal Electoral Institute, which issued voter ID cards, because it was almost impossible to live in Mexico without possessing one. Other than voting, the card was used to open bank accounts, and most merchants asked for it when they sold beer.

"That may take time, sir?"

"I know, but there are other ways of tracking down her family, and I have men getting closer to them as we speak."

After setting his phone down, Alvarado received

another call, and he learned about the death of Enrique De Jesús.

"Tanner, you son of a bitch," Alvarado whispered, and he had to fight the desire to send men to Mexico City to search for Tanner. When the urge passed, he smiled.

Let the bastard and his friends do all the damage they want. Alvarado told himself. He would not split up the force he had at the compound.

Tanner was smart, he did have to give the man that much credit. If he hadn't been warned about the fact that he would be stowed away in a shipping container, the man might have made it inside the compound.

Martinez had given Alvarado the notes the strike team had gathered concerning Tanner's tactics, and the depth of the man's cleverness was impressive. Still, no amount of guile would help Tanner once he was captured. In the meantime, Alvarado wondered what new damage Tanner would inflict upon his business, and he tried to think of where he would strike next.

When the answer came to Alvarado, he felt sick inside, but then dismissed it entirely. There was no possible way that Tanner could know about the facility he was thinking of. Besides, he already had enough security guarding the place to hold off an army.

The facility was not only disguised, but also underground, which made it infinitely more difficult to breach. It was so secure that Alvarado had designated it as a backup refuge in the event that his compound had fallen.

It was located only eight miles away from where Alvarado sat. There were no drugs there, but rather a stockpile of cash, which was just waiting to be laundered or used to buy weapons. The bills were mostly American dollars, but there were also pesos, and their combined value was currently over fifty million.

Alvarado reached for his phone, changed his mind, reached for it again, picked it up, and then placed it back on the desk. Tanner wasn't interested in money. He was in Mexico to seek revenge.

Alvarado spun his chair around and gazed out the patio door. After closing his eyes, he fantasized once more about the atrocious acts of violence he would inflict on Tanner and Spenser. The very thought of it made him shiver with pleasure.

~

As he lay flat on a sand dune, Tanner used a pair of binoculars as he attempted to look at Alvarado's compound, but due to the aperture of the terrain, all he could make out was the top of a wall and the flagpole beyond it.

Behind him was an old structure made of corrugated metal, and to the left of the building and up a hill was a narrow road that saw little traffic.

There were Spanish words handwritten across the front and sides of the building in large letters that when translated read, Ramos Pool Cleaning Service.

Tanner had watched one of the business's ratty white vans return and drive into the building. Except for the fact that it rode low to the ground and seemed wider than a normal van, he never would have suspected the vehicle was armored and transporting cash.

"How did you discover this place, Alexa?" Spenser asked. He was lying on her right, while Tanner was on her left.

The three of them were wearing camouflage outfits like the one Alexa wore the night she breached Alvarado's compound, but in the bright light of an afternoon sun, they were still easy to pick out. The facility they were looking at had both cameras and motion detectors. If they drew too close, their presence would be known.

"I came across it when I was first scouting the compound. I always came at night and thought it strange that there was activity going on here at all hours. Then, when I was in the city, I spotted one of the vans drive into a building I knew housed a drug operation. That's when I realized that the pool trucks were really armored and ferrying cash."

Spenser pointed to a group of poles near the front of the building. "It looks like you were right about their reliance on the cameras. I can also make out several vents leading into the ground. That building is nothing but a prop for what's going on beneath it."

Tanner stared at the structure with an intense gaze as he spoke his thoughts aloud. "We should call Dante for help with this one since we have no idea how many men are down there."

Alexa called his name, breaking his concentration. "Tanner."

"Yes?"

"I would love to break in there and steal that money too, but take it from the daughter of a thief, sometimes it's easier to get inside a place than it is to get out. If we were discovered in there and they sealed it shut, they could take their time hunting us down. We would also need a large vehicle to haul all the money away."

Tanner smiled at her. "You were raised by a thief, but I was mentored by a killer."

Alexa's brow wrinkled in confusion. "What's that mean?"

"It means my concern isn't with the money, but the men who are guarding it."

"You have a plan," Spenser said. "What is it, Cody?"

"It's from the book, and the idea came from Tanner Three. Do you remember how he killed the man hiding in the caves?"

Spenser recalled the tale and smiled.

"What's this about a cave?" Alexa asked, and Spenser explained.

"Tanner Three once took a contract on a guy who had gone up into the hills to hide. The man had lived there as a boy and knew his way around the caves that were in the area. They weren't deep caves or very big, but they were all connected. If you didn't know your way around inside them, it could take some time to find a way out. Tanner Three pretended to be making a delivery, but the man grew wary of him and rushed into a cave."

Alexa looked over at Tanner. "So, how did he kill the man?"

"He had arrived in a truck hauling kerosene and came upon the target while the man was chopping wood. After the man entered the caves, Tanner Three used the axe on the truck to chop a hole in the tank. Once the kerosene had leaked out and run down into the cave, he set it on fire. He later found the target leaning against a tree and struggling to breathe; the man had avoided the fire, but not the fumes."

Alexa considered the story, but then shook her head. "That underground chamber isn't a cave system, and I would be surprised if it wasn't airtight. Even if we flooded the building with gasoline it might not leak down below."

Tanner pointed at the nest of cameras. "What do you think would be the response if they saw a carload of men follow one of their vans onto the property?"

"They would send up a force to deal with it."

"Right, and to come up, they would need to create an

opening, an opening that would allow the gas to enter the chamber."

Alexa gazed over at the building and smiled. "Let's do it."

24

BURN BABY, BURN

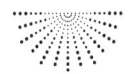

THE GYM OWNER THAT SYLVIA HAD TOLD THE FEDERALES to see owned a small chain of health clubs. Once she saw the federal credentials, she told them everything she knew about Alexa.

"I first met her at my newest club in San Juan Del Rio. She would work out there whenever she visited her father for more than a day or two."

"Her father lives in San Juan Del Rio?"

"Yes, but I never met him. I just dropped her off there when her car wouldn't start."

"Do you remember the address?"

"No, but you can't miss it. It's right at the top of a hill, and I can give you directions."

∼

TANNER JUMPED FROM THE CAB OF A SEMI-TRAILER THAT held over six thousand gallons of gasoline. They had called Dante and told him they needed assistance. When they revealed what they had planned, Dante told them they were mad to even consider burning up that much cash. He then agreed to help, with the understanding that any money salvaged would be his alone.

Tanner said yes, and then told Dante what they needed and how they would do it.

The assault on the underground compound was ready to begin after Dante arrived with the fuel truck, four men he could trust, and two police officers that he owned.

They had staged an accident between the fuel truck and one of two pickups they were using, and the "accident" blocked the road just past the entry to the building's parking lot.

That was followed by the appearance of the cops, and while they exited their patrol car and pretended to investigate the accident, more of Dante's men arrived in a second pickup truck.

The second pickup was driving along behind one of the pool service vans. When it followed the van into the parking lot, an overhead door on the building rolled up to let the van inside, even as two men with rifles emerged from the building.

The pickup drove to the edge of the property where its riders exited the vehicle while brandishing their own weapons. That was when Tanner started the truck and steered it toward the building.

∼

THE TRUCK WAS ROLLING ALONG AT A SEDATE NINE MILES AN hour when Tanner made his leap, but it quickly picked up speed as it left the highway and rolled down the sandy hill at the side of the corrugated building.

At one point, the truck rammed into a sand dune and Tanner thought it might come to a stop. But no, the hill was steep enough, and the truck heavy enough to ensure forward momentum.

However, hitting the dune had altered the truck's direction, and it soon became apparent that it would miss the building altogether.

It did so, but by less than three feet. After slamming into and then climbing onto a set of concrete benches which were near the metal poles that held the nest of cameras, the truck tipped, wobbled, and then crashed onto its side. Ironically, it fell onto a fire hydrant, which punched a hole in the side of the tank. The hydrant was one of two, with the second one located at the rear of the property.

They were fed from a line of water tanks that were positioned along the parts of the desert that had a higher elevation, such as the few buttes in the area. When combined, the tanks formed a water main that could be tapped at the hydrants.

The Alvarado compound had more hydrants behind its walls that employed the system, and at one time, Alexa had considered using the water as a way to poison Alvarado and his men.

She soon abandoned that idea when she discovered that the water was also used by the surrounding ranches in the area. The water was needed primarily for irrigation and not for drinking, and Alvarado shipped in bottled water for himself and his people.

Gasoline soon flowed from the wreck, and because of the grading of the parking lot, it all flowed directly toward the building.

A dozen more men appeared from the building, most of them had shotguns, but two of them were carrying M60 machine guns. Tanner, Alexa, and Spenser began cutting the men down with their long-range rifles, even as Dante and his group fired on them from behind their two pickups.

The cops that had arrived with Dante were the only ones not involved in the firefight. They took cover behind their patrol car, which was above the property and parked on the road.

It was the cops' responsibility to keep an eye out for any approaching traffic on the quiet road and, in particular, any vehicles coming from the direction of Alvarado's desert compound.

When a stray spark from the engine of the truck ignited the fuel, it also set ablaze the surviving men who had come out of the building, even as the fire entered the chamber below.

The remaining group of Alvarado's people who were still underground must have spent time attempting to douse the flames, because it took several minutes for the first one to come out. The man climbed up from a stairway. The entrance had been hidden beneath the sand thirty meters from the building. As soon as he was on the surface, he ran off at a sprint toward Alvarado's compound while shouting into a cell phone.

Tanner raised his rifle, but then decided to let the man live. If the crew down below hadn't already contacted Alvarado, then the fleeing man could tell Alvarado all about the raid on his cash depot. Either way, it was too late to do anything about it now.

The second man to emerge held a gun in his hand, but he was choking on the fumes from the fire in the chamber. When Dante told him to drop the weapon, the man did so, then he reached back to help one of his fellow workers climb out, a woman.

A great black plume soon filled the sky. It was fed by the burning of a fortune in ill-gotten gain.

Two of Dante's men had braved the building and made it out with the pool service van they had followed onto the property. It held nearly a million in bundled cash; the bills were held together by rubber bands.

Dante rewarded his men by tossing several packets to each of them, and even the cops, who had stayed out of the action, drifted over to wet their beaks.

Dante stared inside the van at the pile of cash that was left and said that he knew just how to spend it so that it would do the most good. He would use it to recruit more men from the villages.

Tanner looked at his watch. "It's almost time to rendezvous with Amy and Alexa's father. Why don't we tell Dante the rest of our plan now?"

Dante had been standing nearby. He turned and looked at Tanner.

"What's this you're talking about?"

They told him, while leaving out the most important part, but Dante understood that they trusted him about as much as he trusted them. Still, for now, their goals were in alignment, and Dante told them he would do as they asked.

"Just remember," Tanner said. "That delivery truck has to reach the compound at its scheduled time, twelve noon, and the crate has to be on it."

"I'll take care of it," Dante said. "But these changes you're making, I don't see how they will help you kill Alvarado."

Alexa told him that it would all make sense in the end and Dante shrugged. He knew he was in so deep that he had to see things through. Within twenty-four hours he would either be in control of Alvarado's cartel or be hunted for betraying his boss, Damián Sandoval.

Eight of Alvarado's people survived the firefight and

the smoke, not counting the man who had run off. They were six men and two women.

Tanner walked over to them. They were down on their knees and had their hands secured behind their backs.

Tanner pointed at the ones on the left. "These three will do."

25
TRAPPED

Amy was sitting on the steps of Rodrigo's home and wishing for the man and his companion to appear. She had the rental parked in front of the house and facing the nearby cross street, so that they could drive away as soon as possible once Rodrigo showed.

Scar, Bruise, Wound, and Abrasion were down along different sections of the hill keeping watch. If they saw anyone in a vehicle who looked shady, they would give Amy a call. Few cars came or went up the hill, as it was the middle of a workday, but each time one approached, Amy felt dread. By two o'clock, Amy had begun to pace in front of the house. When her phone rang, and she saw that it was Scar, she was certain that he was going to tell her to run and hide among the trees.

"Yes?"

"I think they're finally here," Scar said.

Seconds later, Amy let out a great sigh of relief as she watched the red pickup truck crest the hill and then pull into the driveway. When Emilio stepped out of it, she recognized him immediately.

"Mr. Lucia, my name is Amy. Your daughter Alexa sent me to take you somewhere safe."

Rodrigo looked both worried and suspicious as he helped the blind Emilio out of the passenger seat. "If what you're saying is true, my daughter would have given you a code word to say."

Amy smiled. "Alexa said the code word was 'pony.'"

"That's correct, but is my daughter all right?"

"Yes sir, but Alonso Alvarado wants to hurt her, and Alexa is afraid that he'll come after you as well."

Rodrigo's face paled as the blood drained from it. "Good God."

Amy pointed to her vehicle. "We should leave right away."

"I can't. Emilio ran out of medicine and I must go inside and get the rest of it, along with some important papers and a photo album. I won't leave here without that album; there are pictures in it of Alexa when she was a child."

"All right, but please hurry, and while you're doing that, I'll help your friend into my car."

"I have to pee first," Emilio said, and Amy sighed.

~

ALVARADO STOOD WITH THE HELP OF CRUTCHES ON THE front porch of his home and watched as black smoke rose toward the sky in the distance. That smoke was his money going up in flames.

An hour ago, he would have said that it was impossible to hate Tanner and Spenser any more than he already did. He would have been wrong.

Malena stood beside him. She was so angry that she was trembling. "How much money was kept there?"

"Over fifty million."

Malena stamped her foot. "Why the hell are they burning it?"

"Because Tanner is the devil, and the devil cares nothing for money, only souls."

∼

Scar was coming out of a restaurant that sold ice cream when he saw the Federales drive by him in an official looking vehicle. Following close behind them was a Cadillac Escalade with two huge men in the front seats. He dropped his triple-scooped, chocolate chip mint ice cream cone, fumbled for his cell phone, and called Amy.

"We're coming," Amy said, when she answered. "We've just gotten into the car."

"No, hey, you gotta get out of there. There are four dudes headed your way. They're coming up the hill now."

"Oh no, um, stay away and I'll call you soon."

Amy tossed her phone on the seat, started the engine, and looked lost as to what to do next. The only way to leave the area by car was to drive down the hill, since the other direction ended at a cul-de-sac. There was also the option of abandoning the rental and disappearing into the nearby trees. However, beyond the initial row of decorative ash trees, the land beyond was open and offered scant shelter.

Also, due to Emilio's blindness, Amy doubted they could make it far enough away in time on foot to be out of sight of the men who were hunting them.

Rodrigo spoke from the back seat, where he was sitting beside Emilio. "The men are nearby?"

"Yes."

Rodrigo pointed out the rear window. "Go in reverse

and back into the driveway two doors down. The man that lives there never closes his garage door when he leaves for work in the morning."

Amy did as Rodrigo asked, and yes, the garage was sitting with its door open. It was an attached garage, and it sat at the bottom of a steep incline.

As she backed down into the spot, Amy glimpsed the front of a car appear at the top of the hill, and then she was inside the garage.

Rodrigo hopped out and pulled the door down as Amy killed the engine. A tinny voice could be heard. It was Scar. He had stayed on the line when Amy dropped the phone onto the seat beside her.

"Amy?"

"Hi, we're good. We're hiding inside a neighbor's garage."

"Shit. What do you want us to do?"

Amy hesitated in answering as she heard car doors opening and slamming shut.

"Amy?" Scar said.

"Call the others and tell them to stay away."

"Okay, but how are you going to sneak past those guys?"

"I wouldn't dare try; they might chase us. But listen, I want you four to get a taxi and ride back to the motel."

"What then?"

"I don't know but—"

Amy stopped talking as she heard voices coming from outside. It was the men from the cars, the Federales. They were talking in Spanish and sounded very close.

Amy whispered into the phone. "I can't talk; they're here."

Then, she ended the call, and murmured a prayer.

26

A GAME OF CATCH

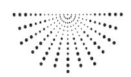

While Alvarado's thugs broke into Rodrigo and Emilio's home, the two Federales paced out on the sidewalk in front of the property. Amy heard them talking when they traveled as far as the home where she, Rodrigo, and Emilio were hiding in the garage.

The men stopped pacing and just stood on the sidewalk. Amy hoped it was just a coincidence they had stopped there, and that they weren't preparing to slide up the garage door.

Her Spanish was just so-so, but she could make out enough to know that they were talking about a series of attacks carried out on Alvarado's people in Mexico City, which was a two-hour drive south. Amy knew the attacks must be the work of Spenser, Tanner, and Alexa, and realized they were still too far away to call for help.

One or both of the men must have been smoking because the scent of the tobacco drifted into the garage. Amy's window was down, and the breeze blew the smell of the cigarettes into the enclosed space.

Emilio sneezed. It was a small sneeze, and he had muffled it with a hand, but the men outside abruptly ended their conversation. When one of the men shouted, Amy feared that they were ordering them to exit the garage. However, the man was shouting for someone to get away from his car, and a moment later, Amy heard the men move back toward Rodrigo's house.

~

The Tin Horsemen were playing with their Frisbee around the cars belonging to the Federales and the thugs. One of the Federales shouted for them to go away.

None of the Horsemen spoke a word of Spanish, but they had been hassled by cops before, and they knew how to piss them off without saying a word. Scar threw a thumb toward the Federale who was shouting at him, as if to say, "Do you believe this guy? He thinks he owns the whole street."

Bruise and Wound laughed loudly at the man, and while that was going on, Abrasion was beneath the vehicle and puncturing the rear tires with a knife.

The other Tin Horsemen kept playing around the cars and laughing while Abrasion skittered on his belly and went beneath the Escalade that belonged to Alvarado's thugs.

He punctured their tires as well, by jamming the blade into the inner wall of the rear wheels, as his friends' raucous laughter masked the sounds of the initial hissing of air. When he was done, Abrasion crawled out from beneath the vehicle, but kept low. When Scar saw that he had finished with the tires, he pretended to make a wild throw with the Frisbee.

The plastic disc flew over the Federales, but since they were closer, they could pick up the toy first, and while they were doing that, Abrasion stood and began walking down the hill, with the other Horsemen following him.

The Federale who had been yelling at Scar turned toward them with a smug look on his face after picking up the Frisbee. He was looking forward to taunting the boys now that he had their toy. The smug look turned to one of surprise when he saw that they were just walking away. He turned and gave his partner a puzzled look.

∽

Amy nearly screamed when her phone rang, and she answered it before it could ring again.

"Yes?" she whispered.

"It's Scar, Amy, get out of there now. Abrasion fucked with their tires, and it won't be long before they notice."

"What?"

"Open that garage door and get out of there. You can pick us up at the bottom of the hill, hurry!"

Amy tossed the phone onto the seat beside her and got out of the car. She flung the garage door open, and when Rodrigo asked her what was going on, she told him that he and Emilio needed to duck down low in their seats.

Rodrigo placed a hand on blind Emilio's back and nudged him to lean over, and as he did that, Amy started the engine.

She sped up the sharp incline of the short driveway and out onto the street, then was taken aback when she saw that the Federales were standing nearby.

The men were too close. They spotted the hunched over forms of Rodrigo and Emilio in the rear seat, and then began shouting to the thugs who were still inside the house.

※

When Amy brought the car to a halt at the bottom of the hill, she stopped so suddenly that Emilio's dark glasses flew off and fell into his lap.

The Tin Horsemen piled into the vehicle as the Federales' car appeared at the top of the hill. Amy took off, leaving rubber behind while glancing nervously in the rearview mirror.

The Feds were coming on, but their car seemed to shimmy, and behind it, a larger vehicle appeared, and it also rode along with a shimmying motion, as if the driver of the vehicle was fighting for control of the steering wheel.

Scar had said that Abrasion had done something to the men's tires; whatever he had done was having an effect.

Amy slowed for safety, but ran a red light, and within seconds she was merging onto the highway. Behind her, her pursuers had fallen back farther as they also navigated the moving cross traffic at the red light. When the men chasing them tried to accelerate to match the flow of traffic on the highway, the shimmying of their vehicles graduated to a wild swaying.

The car driven by the Federales then crossed into the next lane, bounced off another vehicle, overcompensated, and wound up running off the road and into a ditch.

The Escalade kept coming. It had a superior engine and would have normally caught up to Amy with ease, but before long it was throwing off sparks as it rode on its rear rims. Once that happened, Amy's rental grew far out of reach, and with several cars between it and the Escalade.

The thug driving the Escalade faced reality and pulled over.

Scar let out a cheer. "We did it! We got away!"

Rodrigo was smiling at the four boys and asked them who they were.

"They're the Tin Horsemen," Amy said. "And danger is their business."

27
REUNION

When Alexa arrived at the rendezvous point, she let out a cry of joy as she saw Rodrigo and Emilio. After exchanging hugs and kisses, Alexa called over Tanner and Spenser.

Spenser clasped Rodrigo's hand in both of his and told him that it was good to meet him in person.

After shaking Tanner's hand, Rodrigo glanced over at Alexa, and saw how she was looking at Tanner.

"My daughter cares for you, is it mutual?"

"Yes sir," Tanner said. He rarely met the fathers of the women he slept with and felt the less said the better.

He liked Alexa, and yes, he had come to care for her, but he wasn't fool enough to make promises about a future together. For her part, Alexa seemed content to take things as they came.

By noon of the following day, they would be inside Alvarado's compound, inside the belly of the beast. There was no future beyond that in Tanner's mind, not when he was so close to finally achieving payback on the man who had killed his family. With Alvarado dead, then he would make solid plans, plans that included doing what he did best, taking contracts and fulfilling hits.

∽

They were staying the night at a small motel that Damián Sandoval had recently bought and had yet to renovate. From his connections in government, Sandoval had discovered that the roadway outside the motel would soon be part of a new highway, and he had plans to build on to the existing motel while upgrading it.

The place was closed for business, and Dante had left men to guard Tanner and his companions, as he went to finalize the plans that concerned hijacking the delivery truck they would use the next day.

Tanner, Spenser, and Alexa welcomed the reprieve, although thoughts of the danger they would soon face was never far from their minds.

As they all ate dinner together outside around a picnic table, Amy and Scar told of their escape from Alvarado's men.

Alexa rose from her seat and kissed each of the Tin Horsemen on the cheek, and then she hugged Amy where she sat at the table. "Thank you all for saving my Papa Rodrigo and Papa Emilio, I think I would die if anything happened to them."

Emilio rubbed a hand over his white beard as he asked Alexa a question. "Will we ever be able to go home, Alexa?"

Alexa smiled, even though Emilio couldn't see it. "Yes. Once we kill that bastard Alvarado we will all be free to live in peace."

Rodrigo let out a moan. "I'm so worried for you, Alexa."

She went back to her seat beside him and placed an arm over his shoulders. "Look across the table and tell me what you see, Papa."

Rodrigo did so, and saw Tanner and Spenser looking back at him.

"I see two men."

"No, Papa, you see two Tanners, and they are every bit as capable as the Tanner you once knew."

Rodrigo stared at Tanner and Spenser. "If that is true, Alonso Alvarado is already dead and just doesn't know it."

"We'll make him aware of that fact tomorrow," Tanner said, and Rodrigo smiled.

After dinner, they talked for a while, but then Rodrigo and Emilio decided to go to sleep early, because they had to rise at daybreak to say goodbye to Alexa.

The Tin Horsemen drifted from the table after that, while taking a six-pack of beer with them. That left Amy, Tanner, Spenser, and Alexa to go over the details of their plan once more. As they were talking, Spenser noticed that Abrasion was staring over at Amy.

After Tanner and Alexa retired to their room, Spenser told Amy that he would join her shortly. He then drifted over to where the Tin Horsemen were drinking beer and listening to a radio station that played American music.

"Lionel, can I see you for a second?"

Abrasion walked over to him, and Spenser stared into his eyes. "You and I need to talk."

At his compound, Alonso Alvarado stood on crutches atop his porch and looked up at the night sky. Tanner was coming, and would be there tomorrow at noon, when the delivery truck pulled up to the gate.

It was a bold plan Tanner had, and it might have worked if he hadn't been betrayed by Dan Matthews, although the odds were against it. Still, when he gave it some thought, Alvarado saw no other way for Tanner to have made it inside. He had over two-hundred men camped outside the walls of his fortress at all times, and anyone attempting to scale those walls would be easily detected by sight or camera. To even reach the walls, one had to get past the men patrolling the desert.

"Cody Parker," Alvarado whispered, and remembered the boy who had slain eight of his men, two of them while gravely wounded. That boy was a man now, and that man was a killing machine who had never been stopped no matter what force was arrayed against him.

A devil, that was what Rico Nazario had called Tanner and Alvarado thought it was an apt comparison. The devil was coming for him, and he had to be ready.

He saw the man who was in charge of the guards' schedule, and he called him over.

The man, who was ex-military, stood at attention before him.

"Yes sir?"

"When the truck arrives tomorrow, send three more men out to greet it."

Confusion flashed over the man's features. There were already two dozen men picked to meet the truck, but as he had done his whole life, he would follow orders.

"Yes sir. I'll tell the men who normally clean the barracks to be at the truck. Is there anything else, sir?"

"No," Alvarado said, and watched the man march off.

Tanner was coming, and although he would never admit it, not even to himself, Alonso Alvarado was afraid.

∾

THERE WAS SOMEONE ELSE FEARFUL INSIDE THE COMPOUND. It was Martinez.

If things didn't work out the next day, Alvarado would kill him. Everything would have been so much better had Alvarado's people grabbed Alexa Lucia's father to hold as a hostage, but the old man had managed to escape and go into hiding.

When the phone in his pocket vibrated, it startled Martinez, and when he saw who was calling him, he wondered if the news would be good or bad.

"Scar, where the hell have you been?"

"It's not Scar, Martinez, this is Abrasion."

"What, Abrasion? Listen kid, put your friend on the phone."

"Scar doesn't know anything about this call, and he can't. But listen, I can give you Alexa Lucia's father."

"What? How?"

"Didn't Alvarado tell you how the old man got away?"

"Yeah, he said a woman and some kids helped him."

"I'm not a damn kid, but yeah, that was us, and the woman is with the guy who crippled Alvarado. I'll give you her and the old guys, but it won't come cheap."

"How much?"

Abrasion named a figure and heard Martinez gasp.

"You're crazy."

"Talk to Alvarado and see if he thinks I'm crazy; I bet the fucker pays right up."

"Maybe, but tell me something, why are you doing this, just for the money?"

"I have other reasons," Abrasion said.

"All right, call me back in fifteen minutes."

∼

When Abrasion called back, Martinez, on speakerphone, told him that they had a deal. Martinez was in Alvarado's office, and seated across the desk from the drug lord.

"The money will be in your account when the banks open tomorrow," Martinez said. "Now, tell us where we can find the woman and the old men."

Abrasion's laugh was loud over the phone. "Yeah, right, and then the money never shows up. I'll call when I see the cash in the bank, but one more thing."

"What's that?" Martinez asked.

"Um, the lady, don't hurt her, okay?"

"Sure kid, whatever you say, but if you don't make that call, men will be sent to hunt you down and kill you."

"I'll call, but first I see the money."

"You'll see it," Martinez said, then the call ended, and he looked over at Alvarado. "Once we have the woman and the old men, Tanner's fate will be sealed. If you don't kill him, his companions will trade him to get back their loved ones."

Alvarado smiled. He could almost smell Tanner's blood.

PART III
SLEIGHT OF HAND

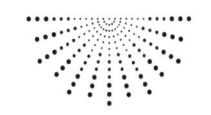

28

LOVE LOST, MONEY GAINED

THE FOLLOWING MORNING, THE SUN ROSE BRIGHT AND HOT on a new day, and for some it would be their last.

Tanner thought it best for the Tin Horsemen to fly back home before the assault on the compound, but he had thanked them for their help.

"You boys are more useful than I would have thought, but why don't you give up trying to be tough guys. It doesn't suit you."

Scar nodded at that. "I think you're right, but we did have fun helping Amy."

Everyone told the boys goodbye, and Amy hugged each of them. When she reached Abrasion, she added a peck on the cheek.

"Have a good flight, Lionel."

"I will, and Amy?"

"Yes?"

Abrasion sighed. "Never mind, it doesn't matter anymore."

The boys left for the airport, and Tanner, Alexa, and Spenser prepared themselves to assault the compound.

∽

Inside an apartment in Mexico City, Dante was holding a gun on a man named Julio. The man was the regular driver of the delivery truck that supplied Alvarado's compound. Two of Dante's men held Julio's wife by her arms, as Dante explained to the young man what he needed him to do.

Julio had looked angry, but that soon morphed into fear, and when he realized that Dante was asking him to cross Alonso Alvarado, he became terrified, and a tear escaped.

"Sir, this man Alvarado, he will kill me; he will kill us all."

Dante sent Julio a smile that looked much more confident than he felt. "Alonso Alvarado will die. You do everything I ask of you and your wife will be returned to you unharmed. Do you understand? Alvarado can't save you or your wife, only I can." Dante gestured to one of his men. "This man will drive you to work. Once you're in your truck and have left the depot you will meet him at a warehouse where you will take on a pallet. From that point on you will do what you normally do, and that means that you will make it to Alvarado's compound by noon. Try to run or call the police and you'll never see your wife again, understood?"

Julio looked like he might vomit, but after swallowing several times, he answered.

"I understand, and I'll do anything to get my wife back. Do not hurt her."

Dante looked at one of his men. "Take him to work, and after the truck is loaded, come to the place I told you."

"This is going to work, isn't it Dante?" the man asked.

"I would bet my life on it," Dante said. "And in fact, I have."

~

Sometime later, at the Mexico City Airport, Abrasion checked to see if Alvarado had sent the money. He had, and Abrasion made a call.

Martinez answered before the first ring had finished sounding off. "You got your money, now, where are they?"

Abrasion gave him the address of the motel, hung up the phone, and went to get on his flight.

29
SPECIAL DELIVERY

When it was time for Tanner, Spenser, and Alexa to separate from Amy, Rodrigo, and Emilio, all six of them knew that there was a chance they would never see each other again.

Realizing a sad fact and giving in to it were two separate things, and Tanner, Spenser, and Alexa spoke with confidence when they said that they would all reunite.

Tanner stood by as Alexa hugged Rodrigo and Emilio, and Spenser held Amy in a warm embrace, but then it was time to leave, and the three of them left the motel.

∼

With the assault on the compound only hours away, Dante had removed most of the guards. The two men that remained at the motel looked to be asleep, as they sat propped up under a tree with their hats pulled down over their faces, and several beer cans were scattered about.

The men Alvarado sent to grab Amy, Rodrigo, and

Emilio, shot the two guards over a dozen times each with silenced weapons, and then strolled past the bodies.

When they broke down the door where the sound of a TV was playing, they saw the frightened woman and two old men, and smiled, for they had just earned the bonus they'd been promised.

When Alvarado, a man who once loved to talk in chess phrases, learned that he had Spenser and Alexa's loved ones, he said three words.

"Checkmate grows near."

~

DANTE'S MAN STOOD BESIDE THE TRUCK DRIVER, JULIO, AS they watched the phony pallet being loaded onto the tractor-trailer. At Dante's orders, his men had removed six wrapped skids that had been stacked high with cases of bottled water, fruit juice, and beer. The discarded pallets sat at the left side of the warehouse.

Julio's eyes had widened in surprise when he saw the two men and the beautiful woman climb inside the hidden opening of the wrapped skid of hollow cartons, and once again, he wondered what madness he had been dragged into.

When the stowaways were on the truck and the back door sealed, Julio climbed into his cab and headed for the compound, a religious man, he prayed as he never had before.

30
SO FAR, SO GOOD

"Get on your knees," Alvarado said, as he glared at Amy, Rodrigo, and Emilio, who had their hands cuffed behind their backs.

The guards pressed down on their shoulders and forced them to do what was commanded. Emilio, his blindness hidden behind dark glasses, nearly fell forward, but he steadied himself and went down to his knees.

Amy was dressed in jeans and a long-sleeved T-shirt, while both Rodrigo and Emilio wore dark suits with white shirts and no ties.

Like many older men, their clothes appeared to be too big for them, something that often happened when age began to wrinkle the flesh and muscle mass diminished. It caused both men to look soft beneath the loose garments.

Malena stood beside her husband and glared at the captives before her, as a triumphant smile sat on her lips.

Amy was staring up at her, while Emilio, blinded, stared straight ahead, and Rodrigo kept his head bowed with his gray-streaked hair hanging down and obscuring his eyes. They were in the courtyard, near the fountain, and the hot sun beat upon them as midday approached.

Alvarado was on his crutches, but he bent over as far as he could and spoke in a voice filled with hate.

"I know all about Tanner's pathetic plan to infiltrate my compound, and I will use the three of you as a weapon against him."

Amy stared up at Alvarado as a tear rolled down her right cheek. Malena saw in her gaze a look of defiance mixed with hate. She walked over to Amy and wrapped a hand around her throat.

"You are the lover of the man who crippled my husband, yes? Then know this, the pain your man caused mine is but a fraction of the agony your man will experience. And someday, I'll come for you as well, just for the hell of it."

Amy said nothing, but the look of defiance faded. It wasn't replaced by fear as Malena had hoped it would be, but rather by concern.

Malena released her, and Alvarado shouted an order to the guards.

"Lock them up!"

As Amy, Rodrigo, and Emilio were being herded away by the guards, Alvarado checked his watch.

"The truck will be here soon."

Malena kissed her husband on the lips. "We will have vengeance."

∼

Although most infractions of the rules within the compound carried a sentence of death, there were a few minor regulations that when broken only resulted in incarceration for a few days.

Those sentences were served in a cell that had a dirt floor two meters square along with a ceiling that was just over six-feet high. The place smelled of feces, urine, and vomit, and underscoring it all was the faint scent of death.

The cell was located near the barracks, and the sun beat down on its metal roof all day. The guards jammed Amy, Rodrigo, and Emilio into the tight space, even as one of them copped a feel of Amy's ass.

When the door slammed shut, the cell became nearly devoid of light, but there was a crack in one of the brick walls, and a thin sliver of daylight illuminated Amy's face.

She smiled as she looked at Rodrigo. "Spenser's plan is working."

31
TURNING TABLES

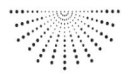

Julio, the young truck driver, was sweating buckets. If not for the love he felt for his wife, he would have abandoned the truck on the side of the road and run off through the desert.

The worst part was that he felt responsible for what was happening. He knew who Alvarado was, knew that the man was a merciless drug lord, a Narco kingpin, but he had volunteered to make the deliveries to the compound every Friday because it paid extra.

There wasn't enough money in the world to replace his sweet wife. If he got out of this mess alive, he promised himself that he would never let money sway his decisions again.

When the compound came into view, he felt his stomach flip at the sight of it. Also, something had happened recently that had caused them to change the configuration of the entry gate. There were also hordes of men camped outside the walls, and as far as Julio could tell, they all held weapons of one kind or another.

Julio thought the man named Dante must be insane to

think that two men and a woman could overcome the odds, but he could plainly see the plan. They hoped to get inside the compound, where there were far fewer men, and then they would strike. It was a wiser move than facing the multitude outside the walls, but there must still be a dozen or more men in the compound, and first, one had to get through both the outer and inner gates.

~

Inside the compound, another young man was sweating from nervousness. It was Joaquin, Dante's friend. He had been busy since learning that an attack was coming and had gained two new allies among Alvarado's men.

Both men were from the local towns and were enraged by the murder of the prostitutes who had been present on the night that Alexa had breached the compound. They were not alone in their feelings, as an undercurrent of hate for Alvarado had been spawned by that heartless act, but the two men were the only ones that Joaquin was willing to trust.

When the attack began, Joaquin and the other two men would be ready to give aid, and if successful, he would signal Dante.

Joaquin heard a shout. One of the tower guards had spotted a vehicle approaching, and the vehicle was a truck.

It's time, Joaquin thought, and then he kissed the silver cross that hung from his neck and prepared himself to kill.

~

Alvarado and Malena watched the truck approach. They were seated in the rear of a large golf cart that was parked near the inner gate. They couldn't see anything outside the walls with the naked eye, but they were each looking at a computer tablet that was receiving a feed from the cameras outside the front gates.

Martinez had driven the golf cart, and he too was watching on a tablet from behind the wheel.

"Finally," he said, hopeful that in mere hours he would be free to leave the compound.

The truck slowed as it approached the first gate leading into the compound, the outer gate, then slowed even faster, as a pickup truck drove in front of it and forced it to stop a dozen yards from the gate.

The man inside the pickup fired several rounds into the front tires of the delivery truck, while also perforating its radiator.

In the truck, Julio dived to the floor of the cab, as his heart beat wildly.

∼

INSIDE THE COMPOUND, ALVARADO SPOKE TO TWO OF THE three guards who were standing near him.

"Bring the hostages here."

Both men answered with a single nod and headed toward the cell.

"Why do you want them?" Malena asked.

"I don't see how Tanner could possibly make it past the gates, but if he does, I'll use the hostages to bargain with. If nothing else, they'll make a handy shield."

On the monitor, the guard from the pickup truck approached the big rig and, after ripping open the door, he screamed at the driver to get out of the cab. Julio complied, and the guard shoved him toward a second guard who had just arrived at the truck with two other men.

One of the men held a thermal imager, while the other held an augmented directional microphone. As the two aimed their instruments at the truck, a group of nearly two dozen men approached the truck's rear.

They were all armed and wearing heavy body armor and bullet resistant helmets, and each looked as if they were expecting the truck to be filled with live tigers.

The man with the thermal imager appeared stymied by what he was seeing, and he reported that because the inside temperature of the truck was so high due to the day's heat, that he couldn't distinguish any forms from the ambient air.

However, the second man, the man with the microphone confirmed that he was hearing three heartbeats.

"They're calm, all three of them," said the man. "A nice steady rhythm."

Alvarado heard the man's words and made a face. "The devil doesn't feel fear, but I'm sure he feels pain, use the gas."

On screen, two men forced open the rear doors of the trailer while another man lobbed tear gas inside. After the doors were shut again, the man with the directional microphone spoke.

"Their heartrates have risen, and I can hear coughing."

Alvarado gave the order to enter the trailer and drag them out.

∼

The two guards sent to get Amy, Rodrigo, and Emilio didn't even bother to take out their guns before opening the door on the cell. Their captives were an unarmed woman and two old men, one of which was blind, and all three of them had their hands cuffed behind their backs.

Once the door opened, their captive's eyes blinked at the sudden light, that is, those eyes that could still see.

"Come out," said one of the guards.

Amy went first. As she came even with the guards, Emilio refused to budge and began cursing at them. He was joined by Rodrigo.

As they were getting the guards attention, Amy slipped behind the men, and in a flash of movement, she jammed a thin round blade into each man's back, while aiming for their kidneys.

Both guards cried out in agony. One man took a swing at Amy, who ducked beneath it, as the other man put his hand on his weapon. Before he could slide the gun from its holster, Rodrigo grabbed his wrist, and at the same time, he drove the palm of his hand at the man's face on an upward angle, breaking the guard's nose.

Amy still held the short thin knives. She sliced a line across the man's throat and ended the movement by jamming one of the blades into his Adam's apple. The guard collapsed to his knees with both hands to his throat, and Rodrigo took his weapon.

While that was going on, Emilio was on the ground with the other guard, and he had the man in a choke hold. With one hand, the man was clawing at the sleeve of Emilio's suit jacket in an attempt to break the hold, while with his other hand, he tried to free his weapon from the holster, but Emilio had a leg wrapped around the man's waist, preventing him from grabbing the gun.

After an audible, *SNAP!* the man went limp, and Emilio flung him aside. When he stood, he looked down at the other guard just in time to see him take his last breath, as he lay on the ground with a gashed and bloody throat.

Emilio took hold of something that was hanging around his neck, beneath his shirt. After lowering his head and removing the dark glasses, he slid an eye patch up into place.

Emilio was actually Spenser. He was wearing makeup along with stipple latex to make his face and hands look wrinkled and darker, while his hair and beard were dyed white. Rodrigo, who was Tanner, was similarly made up.

Amy was Alexa, and while she hadn't any need to look older, she wore makeup on her arms, face, neck, and hands, to pass as Caucasian. A pair of blue contact lenses completed her look.

The real Amy, a former professional makeup artist, had practiced on getting their disguises just right while they were still in Wyoming. She was able to apply the makeup in a matter of hours before leaving with Rodrigo and Emilio to a secure location that morning.

Expecting to be taken hostage, Tanner, Spenser, and Alexa had hidden handcuff keys on themselves. They used the one from inside the hollow heel of Alexa's shoe to get free of the cuffs.

The two thin blades were from "Emilio's" dark eyeglasses. They were clipped to the inside of the glasses' frame, along the arms.

The blades were the length of the arms, while the curved earpieces were the small handles. Although they were only a few inches long, the knives were rigid and razor sharp.

The men killed at the motel, and who were believed to be guards, had actually been two of Alvarado's own people. They were survivors from the raid on the underground vault. Dante had drugged the men and placed them beneath the tree.

Abrasion's seeming betrayal was also part of Spenser's plan. Dante had originally been chosen to play the part of the betrayer. However, Spenser later realized the opportunity for gain from the charade and thought that the Tin Horsemen should profit for all the help they had given, and Abrasion had played the part well.

Alvarado was a man who liked to use his enemies' loved ones as weapons against them. Spenser turned that sick trait back against him. It would soon be the man's downfall.

Tanner checked the guard's weapon, verified that it was loaded, and looked first at Alexa, and then Spenser.

"Let's go kill that motherfucker."

32
LET THE RIGHT ONES IN

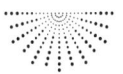

Four men wearing body armor entered the trailer with gas masks on and stun guns at the ready. Alvarado ordered that the captives be taken alive, and so the men carried no lethal weapons.

The sound of coughing was coming from the first wrapped skid on the right, and it was shaking from the movement within it.

Once they examined it, they saw how the phony skid of materials opened. After removing the top, they dragged their prisoners out of the truck and into fresh air. The two men and the woman were coughing violently from the teargas, but it was their appearance that startled everyone.

"They're Mexican, and not just the woman," Malena said. "Alonso, what is going on?"

Martinez looked closely at the image on his screen. The trio were coughing from the gas, yes, but their eyelids drooped as well.

"I think they've been drugged," Martinez said.

One of the men outside said something to the man

who was in communication with Alvarado, and he relayed it.

"Jesús says that he knows these people. He said that they work for you."

Alvarado ordered that the camera zoom in closer, and when it did so, he cursed.

"That woman, she works inside the underground vault counting money. Tanner must have kidnapped them when he destroyed the facility yesterday."

Malena looked uneasy, and she jumped when her husband gripped her wrist.

"What is that on the side of your hand?" Alvarado asked her.

Malena flipped her right hand over and looked. There was something there on the outside of her palm; it was light in color. When she touched it, it felt slippery, and yet powdery at the same time.

"I think it's makeup," Malena said. "I must have gotten it on me when I grabbed the woman earlier."

Alvarado stared at her hand, and in a flash of insight he understood what had happened, and how he had been deceived, so monstrously deceived.

He raised his hands and clamped them to his head as if he were about to pull his hair from its roots.

"Two men and a woman, and like a fool I brought them inside the compound."

"What are you talking about, Alonso?"

Alvarado ignored Malena's question and shouted to a guard who was standing nearby. "Open the gates! Do it now, now!"

The guard said, "Yes sir," and headed toward the inner gate, as Alvarado poked Martinez hard in the ribs with one of his crutches.

"Drive us back to the house, hurry!"

Martinez looked flustered, and barely managed to start the golf cart before the first shot came.

The bullet struck the guard who had been heading to open the gate. His blood sprayed so violently from the exit wound that some of it splattered Malena's white silk blouse.

The cart began moving as more shots rang out, Alvarado turned his head and saw the two guards standing near the gate go down.

Assuming that the guards sent to bring the prisoners were dead, that meant that he had lost five of them, and there were less than a dozen more inside the compound.

He had been concerned with keeping Tanner outside the walls, and so had constantly fortified the forces guarding the walls and the gates. Now, if those gates couldn't be opened, all those men were locked outside and essentially useless.

Alvarado jerked his head back around as a scream came from the left. He watched, horrified, as a tower guard plummeted to the ground. The wounded man landed with a sickening thud. The impact cracked the man's head open and exposed his brains. His eyes looked toward Alvarado, eyes that were empty and dead.

Malena grabbed Alvarado's arm with an iron grip and spoke in a high voice that was laced with fear.

"What is happening?"

"Tanner," Alvarado answered, "It's Tanner."

~

AFTER KILLING THE GUARDS OUTSIDE THEIR CELL, TANNER, Spenser, and Alexa headed for the front gate.

They had to keep it from opening or they would soon find themselves vastly outnumbered. Dante was in the area with his troop of villagers, but unless he received a signal from the young guard, Joaquin, he wouldn't risk approaching the compound.

They made it toward the front wall while being surprised at how empty the compound seemed to be. They had seen the hordes of men outside the walls as they were being brought in and were aware that their enemies numbered in the hundreds.

They peeked around the corner of the compound's large garage, where a line of tall white propane tanks was lined up against the side of the building.

The gate was ahead and to their left, and near it was Alvarado, seated inside a golf cart and looking down at a tablet computer.

"That man driving the cart, he looks like the photo of Martinez that Burke sent us. We need to keep him alive if we can," Tanner said.

Alvarado suddenly appeared as if he had been hit with an electric shock, and then he reached up and grabbed his head. When Tanner saw the look of stunned realization lighting the man's face, he knew what had just happened.

"He's figured it out. Alvarado knows we're here."

"Kill that guard he's talking to," Alexa said. "I'll claim his weapon and go after Alvarado while you and Spenser secure the gates."

Alexa only had one of the small blades as a weapon, but she had planned all along to seize the gun of the next guard they killed.

When Tanner fired and killed the man walking away from Alvarado, she rushed from concealment and went to claim the man's weapon. Tanner watched her sprint toward the golf cart as Martinez put the machine in motion, then he and Spenser ran toward the inside gate.

~

THE DEAD GUARD WORE A CLIP-ON HOLSTER; ALEXA RIPPED it off his belt and began running after the golf cart, as behind her, she heard the screams of two more dying guards.

A flash of metal caught her attention from above and she brought the gun up and fired. Her hurried shot nearly missed the guard in the watch tower, but she hit him on the side of his head, just above the ear. After dropping his rifle, the man stumbled forward, flipped over the waist high railing, and plummeted to the ground.

On the night she had infiltrated the compound, Alvarado's late brother-in-law, Carlos Ayala, had told her that Alvarado had a safe room in his office, and that it was hidden behind the bathroom wall. Alexa ran as fast as she was able. Alvarado could not be allowed to find shelter, even temporary shelter.

She had waited most of her life to kill him and she would not be delayed in enjoying that pleasure, not when she was so close to delivering retribution. Alexa ran on, and the golf cart being driven by Martinez grew ever closer to the house.

~

TANNER WAS ABOUT TO SHOOT A GUARD WHO WAS TRYING to unlock the inner gate, when he saw the man go down from a head wound. The fatal shot had come from above, and when he looked up, he saw Joaquin waving at him from a guard tower. The body of a dead guard was slumped over the railing beside Joaquin, and there was a knife sticking from its back.

Joaquin pointed at his head, and Tanner saw that he

was wearing a makeshift headband. It was a strip torn from a white sheet and tied around his head.

When Joaquin held up three fingers, Tanner understood that Joaquin was telling him that there were three of them working against Alvarado inside the compound, and that they could be identified by the white headbands.

Tanner signaled that he understood and then shouted the knowledge to Spenser, who was hunkered down behind a jeep and having a firefight with a guard in another tower. That guard soon left the fight, as one of Joaquin's fellow bandana wearers climbed up into the tower and shot him.

Spenser called over to Tanner. "Go help Alexa!" When Tanner didn't move, Spenser saw the conflict in his eyes. "I'll be fine."

Tanner headed for the house. Behind him, Spenser checked his weapon and saw that he was down to only one bullet.

Two guards rounded the corner of the garage with their weapons up. When they spotted Spenser, they took aim at him.

Spenser fired first. He had aimed for one of the propane tanks that were lined up against the wall. The tank punctured at eye level and sent out a spray of cold gas that temporarily blinded the men.

Spenser dropped flat and scrambled beneath the jeep, then kept going until he reached the body of a fallen guard. The man's gun held eight rounds, and Spenser was back in the fight.

∽

Martinez brought the golf cart to a hard stop at the front steps of the house.

Malena had placed a foot on the ground when she spotted Alexa running toward them. Alexa was still far away, but she was coming on fast. "That bitch escaped, Alonso, and so has one of the old men. He's running up behind her and... I've never seen an old man move so fast."

"He's wearing a disguise, they all were, and like an idiot I brought them inside the gates."

Malena gasped. "You mean that old man is actually Tanner... oh my God."

Alvarado grabbed Martinez' arm as the man tried to leave the golf cart. "Drive around to the side of the house where my office is; we'll enter through the patio doors. I have a safe room there."

Malena turned around on her seat to stare at Alexa and shouted a warning. "She's getting closer and so is Tanner!"

Alvarado kept a small gun in his pocket, a .32 Seecamp. He took it out and aimed at Alexa. He had only a slim chance of hitting her, given how far away she was, but he hoped to slow her down. He fired all five shots that the small pistol held.

Three of them fell short, the fourth went wide, and the final round struck Alexa. It hit her on the left, just below the ribs and caused the white T-shirt to blossom red.

To Alvarado's dismay, Alexa merely slowed for a moment as a look of pain crossed her disguised features, but she never stopped running. He dropped the gun and slammed his palm against Martinez's back.

"Go, go!"

The cart took off, and once again, they put distance between themselves and Alexa. When they reached the patio, Martinez had to help Malena get Alvarado to the sliding door. The door was constructed with bullet-resistant glass and would only open once Alvarado's thumbprint was verified. They practically carried Alvarado to the door and held him up; there was no time for him to hobble along on his crutches.

The biometric lock recognized his thumbprint and clicked open. Malena slid the heavy door aside with her left hand as she struggled to hold her husband up with her right.

When Malena looked back, she saw Alexa, and then Tanner, rounding the corner of the house, and she cried out in fear.

Malena, her husband, and Martinez, all tried to squeeze through the opening at the same time. It was a tight fit, but they finally forced their way inside, where Martinez stumbled, taking Alvarado and Malena with him down to the floor.

The door was designed to slide shut on its own, and once closed, it would lock automatically.

Alvarado, Malena, and Martinez laid on the floor and stared back at the patio door as it slid to the right along its track. To each of them it felt as if the door were barely moving.

Alexa could be seen beyond the glass. She was running and firing her gun at the same time as she drew closer. Her rounds missed the narrowing gap of open space between the door and its frame, and instead, they ricocheted off the bullet-resistant glass. When her weapon was empty, Alexa collapsed on the ground against the golf cart, while both exhausted and bloody from the chase.

Then, Tanner appeared, still in his guise of an old and gray-haired man but moving with the grace of a panther. When he was still more than thirty feet from the door, Tanner launched himself into the air. He landed hard on the outer edge of the patio, slid across its white tiled floor, and jammed his gun hand between the patio door and its frame, which kept the door from closing.

Alvarado stared down the barrel of the gun pointed at his face, then, he locked eyes with Tanner, saw the intense glare of hatred within them, and understood that he would soon be dead.

33
THE END OF THE BEGINNING

Joaquin signaled Dante by raising a sheet up the flagpole, and the white linen billowed in the hot desert air, where it could be seen for miles.

With that done, Joaquin climbed up into one of the guard towers, where he used a loudhailer to talk to the men gathered outside the walls.

"The Alvarado cartel is over," Joaquin began, and although he was young, he was well liked, and the men listened.

~

Tanner turned from the patio door and walked back to stand beside Spenser, who was standing next to Alexa. They had all removed their makeup, but Tanner's hair was still dyed with streaks of gray, while Spenser's hair and beard were white.

Alexa's gunshot wound, although bloody, was not serious. Alvarado's bullet had sliced open her skin but hadn't hit muscle or bone. Tanner had bandaged the horizontal wound with layers of gauze to stop the bleeding, and although she felt the effects of the blood loss, Alexa was well.

As she stared at Alvarado, Alexa held a long carving knife she'd taken from the kitchen, and there was a look of triumph on her face.

Alvarado was seated several feet in front of his desk with his wrists handcuffed to his special chair. Seated beside him was Malena, while Martinez was in another room, where he sat alone in a corner.

Tanner had told Martinez to sit there until he said otherwise, and Martinez wisely obeyed.

"My name is Alexa Cazares," Alexa said as she glared down at Alvarado. "And I was there when you killed my family."

Alvarado's eyes grew large with amazement, but then he nodded in understanding.

"You are the one who made the screams I heard coming from the house."

"Yes, I was seven-years-old, and I watched as you and your men destroyed my world."

Alvarado cocked his head, as curiosity overrode the trepidation he was feeling. "How did you survive?"

"I was saved by a man who is a thousand times better than you are, and after saving me, he raised me as his daughter."

Alvarado looked at Tanner as a sneer twisted his face. "And you, Cody Parker, how did you survive?"

Tanner placed a hand on Spenser's shoulder. "He saved me, and we're here now because of his plan."

"I knew you couldn't resist using innocents as pawns," Spenser said, "I also realized you would consider a young woman and two old men no threat to you."

Alvarado went to reach for his wife's hand but was stopped by the handcuff on his wrist.

"Let my wife live. She has harmed no one."

Alexa laughed without a trace of humor. "Do you think we don't know what this bitch is, the things she's done? She also threatened to torture me earlier. How did she put it? 'Just for the hell of it.' No Alvarado, you will find no mercy here."

Malena sprang from her chair while screaming and lunged at Alexa, with hands that were bent like claws.

Alexa stood her ground and made an arc with the knife.

Malena stumbled backwards, missed the chair, and fell to the floor with her hands to her throat. Blood began seeping between her fingers and Alvarado fought against the cuffs while shouting his wife's name.

In a voice that sounded as cold as the grave, Alexa spoke to him. "Now you know what it feels like to see a loved one die."

Alvarado's face was twisted in a rictus of pain and helplessness as he watched his wife perish. Malena's final act was to reach a bloody hand toward Alvarado, but then her arm fell to the carpet, and after a wheeze escaped her, she lay still.

Alvarado turned his eyes from his wife's body and cursed Alexa as he thrashed about in the chair. When he finally wound down, his wrists were bleeding from the friction of the cuffs.

Alvarado slumped in his seat from both exhaustion and resignation of his fate.

Alexa walked over and stood before Alvarado with the knife aimed at his heart, and then she looked back at Tanner.

"Come here and place your hand atop mine, Cody."

Tanner did so, and realized that Alexa had never used his true name before.

They held the knife together and stared down at the man who had altered their lives, and who, in many ways, was responsible for what they were and who they had become.

"This is for my family," Alexa said, "and especially my sweet abuela, my grandmother."

"And for my family as well," Tanner said.

Alexa locked eyes with Tanner, and then they plunged the knife deep into Alvarado's chest.

Alonso Alvarado straightened in his chair as he raised his head and stared at them with a look of defiance, but then he seemed to wilt, as his punctured heart stopped beating. Tanner saw the light leave his eyes, before they closed forever.

Alexa released the blade that was still embedded deep in Alvarado, and then she fell into Tanner's arms, while crying.

Spenser drifted from the room, leaving the two of them alone, and went in search of a phone to call Amy.

34
A NEW DAY

Joaquin's speech won over the hearts of some men, but a group formed to attempt to breach the gates. They failed miserably, and two men were injured when they rammed a small cargo truck against the stout outer gate.

When several other men managed to secure a rope to one of the rear guard towers, they made it over the wall. They had been seen by the cameras as they worked, and Tanner greeted their arrival with death.

Tanner was beginning to wonder if Damián Sandoval had become aware that Dante was planning to take Alvarado's place and had killed him, because six hours passed after Joaquin had raised the sheet aloft on the flagpole, and Dante had yet to show.

But then Dante arrived an hour before sunset, and as he said he would, he had an army of townspeople with him. They arrived in a parade of old vehicles, most of which were used on the local ranches.

The townspeople weren't bearing arms, but rather cases of bottled water. The wise Dante, an ex-resident of the compound, knew that there was no source of water beyond the walls. He had delayed his arrival to let their water supply run out, and then waited even longer while the hot sun did its work on Alvarado's men.

Once Dante had satisfied their thirst, he went about fulfilling their equally innate need to be led. In a commanding tone, Dante shouted for Joaquin to open the gates. Joaquin obeyed, let the men in, and they all got their first look at Alvarado's corpse.

Tanner had propped the body up near the inner gate, in Alvarado's special chair, with the knife still protruding from its chest.

Dante strode up to the chair and gave the corpse a hard kick, which sent it falling to the dirt.

A great silence ensued, followed by a loud cheer that came from the men and the townspeople, and the Alvarado cartel was no more.

~

It was nearing midnight as Tanner, Spenser, and Alexa stood by a Mercedes that had belonged to Malena Alvarado.

The vehicle was a marvel of technology and style, a Mercedes S600 Maybach, and there were less than a thousand miles on it.

Martinez was already in the rear of the car with his wrists cuffed and his ankles bound. Tanner contacted Burke and was told that a man would meet him in Mexico City to take Martinez off his hands.

Tanner had learned of Dan Matthews' treachery from Martinez and had relayed the news to Burke. Burke assured him that someone would see to the matter.

"What's that mean? Have you hired another hitter?"

"No. In fact, I'll hand the job over to the person that recommended you be contacted in the first place."

"And who would that be? Matthews wouldn't say."

"Neither will I, just know that you have an advocate in my corporation."

When Burke brought up the subject of Tanner taking a contract, Tanner told him that he was interested, but needed to decompress.

"I'll be in touch, Burke."

The truck driver, Julio, was going with them as well, to be reunited with his wife in Mexico City. Dante had even given the young man a bundle of cash for his trouble, while telling him that he could come to work for him as a courier.

Julio declined, but when Dante told him how much he would be making, Julio changed his mind and told him yes.

He had forgotten all about the promise he had made to himself to never again let greed cloud his judgement. But he was young, and some lessons had to be learned more than once.

Dante offered his hand and Tanner shook it, as he asked a question.

"You will do that last favor for me, correct?"

"Absolutely, but then we are even."

"Fine by me," Tanner said. "I'm just glad that the bounty is off my head, although it may take time for the word to get out."

Dante laughed. "You forget, this is the computer age, and what happened here today is the stuff of legends. No one will be more surprised than Damián Sandoval that you were successful. And I warn you, he may hold you partly responsible for my rise to power."

"I'll handle Sandoval if it becomes a problem," Tanner

said. "But after seeing what happened to Alvarado, I've a feeling he'll behave."

Dante turned to Alexa and smiled. "Stay here with me and become my queen."

Alexa laughed. "You'll do fine without me. Not only are you in charge, but the locals love you."

"Alvarado ruled with fear, I won't, because I don't want to rule anything. I just want to make money."

Spenser opened the rear door on the Mercedes to climb in beside Martinez and Julio. "So long, Dante, and take care of that kid, Joaquin."

"Joaquin is no kid. He proved that today," Dante said.

"That's true," Spenser said, and got in the car.

They were three miles from the compound when Alexa saw by the round clock set in the dashboard that it was midnight. She was seated up front with Tanner, who was driving.

Alexa pointed out the time to Tanner. She then leaned across the center console, while being careful not to press against her wound, and kissed him gently on the lips.

"It's a new day."

"At last," Tanner said, and they put Alonso Alvarado behind them forever.

PART IV
AFTERMATH

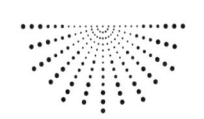

35
TANNER

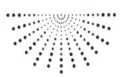

THREE DAYS LATER, NEW YORK CITY

Bosco looked with suspicion at the swarthy Mexican man holding the white box with the red ribbon wrapped around it. Bosco was standing in the doorway of an office building that the Giacconi Family used as temporary headquarters.

On paper, the building was owned by a law firm in Texas, but in truth, the property had belonged to the late Alonso Alvarado.

Joe Pullo, the leader of the Giacconi Family, made a deal with the devil in order to have peace and keep his loved ones safe. The deal made Rico Nazario Joe's partner, but that was when Alvarado, Rico's boss, still lived.

"Who sent you?" Bosco asked the man.

"Dante Cardoso, but I am here on behalf of Tanner."

"Tanner?"

"Yes, you know this name?"

"Yeah," Bosco said, and this time when he looked at

the box, there was a smile spreading across his face. "Get on in here and wait in the lobby. I gotta call my boss."

~

Twenty minutes later, Joe Pullo, Bosco, and Sammy Giacconi entered Rico Nazario's office.

Rico was holding his phone to his ear and had a confused look on his face.

He had heard nothing from Mexico in nearly a week, which he normally would consider to be a good thing, but he had just spent the last five minutes trying to get in contact with Alonso Alvarado and had no success, nor would he, unless he knew a truly gifted spirit medium.

Bosco leaned in the doorway, while Sammy lowered himself onto a white leather sofa, where he stretched out his broken leg with the cast on it.

Joe Pullo walked over to the desk and sat the still unopened box on top of it.

Rico looked around the room. He didn't like the little smile Bosco wore, nor the gaze of Sammy's cold eyes.

"What is this, Joe, a gift?"

"Yeah, and it's from Tanner."

Rico looked confused. "The last I heard of Tanner, he had been seriously wounded in Oklahoma City, likely as he tried to flee into Canada to escape Alonso."

Joe grinned. "Your info is old. Tanner made it to Mexico."

"He did?"

"Um-hmm, now why don't you open that box?"

Rico stared at the box for a few moments and then he stood and slid the carton closer.

"It's almost cold," Rico said.

"I'm guessing that's dry ice," Bosco said. "It keeps things from spoiling."

Rico swallowed, and then carefully undid the ribbon. After slitting the tape on the box with a gold letter opener, he opened it and looked inside.

There was a foam container within. After a long moment of hesitation, Rico removed the lid from the container and stared down at the severed head of Alonso Alvarado.

Rico fell into his seat hard. The impact caused the office chair to slide backwards, where it bumped into the wall behind him.

Rico muttered to himself. "A devil, the man is an absolute devil." After catching his breath, Rico sent Joe a shaky smile. "You were right, Joe. That Tanner… the man is unstoppable."

"You know what this means, don't you, Rico?" Joe said.

And when Rico looked over at Bosco and Sammy, he saw that they were both holding weapons.

~

PANAMA, CENTRAL AMERICA

DAN MATTHEWS WAS LAID OUT ON A KING-SIZE BED INSIDE a luxurious beachfront cabana. The sun was setting, and through the window, Matthews could see it slowly drop toward the blue water.

The cabana, as well as the entire island was rented.

Matthews was in the process of finding the right parcel of waterfront property to buy, and although the island was small, he liked it a great deal. Thanks to the money he had received from Alonso Alvarado, he could afford to buy it.

He was still waiting for a second payment to be deposited into his account but had assumed from the beginning that Alvarado would cheat him. It was why he'd asked for most of the three million dollars upfront, when he sold out and betrayed Tanner.

Matthews had no doubts about Tanner being dead, since Alvarado knew the assassin's plans to infiltrate the compound. Matthews also felt no guilt over the matter.

Tanner was a dirt bag as far as Matthews was concerned. Just a common criminal and a gun for hire. And to think that the U.S. Government was considering using the man to carry out what would essentially be missions to protect national interests.

It irked Matthews that the government was outsourcing wet work. Why have trained military snipers and espionage organizations if you were going to hand all the tough jobs to street thugs?

Matthews sighed heavily. That was all behind him now and the government and Conrad Burke could play their games without him. He was retired and would be living a life of leisure until there was no more life to live.

Matthews drifted off to sleep while watching the sun set; it was just another day in paradise.

~

Paradise ended when the two burly men woke Matthews with a hard slap and tied him to the bed. The men were strangers, but Matthews knew the woman who had come with them; she had been his colleague at the Burke Corporation. She was also the one who had convinced Burke that he needed to hire Tanner.

Matthews had betrayed Burke, while also selling out Tanner and giving Alonso Alvarado vital information. He figured that the woman wanted payback for Tanner's death.

When she informed Matthews that not only was Tanner still alive, but that the man had killed Alvarado, Matthews looked astonished. Then, he asked a question from a mouth that had suddenly gone dry.

"Is Tanner coming here?"

"No, Mr. Burke told Tanner that he would handle you. He sent me after you to keep that promise. Now why not make it easy on yourself and tell me where you've deposited the money?"

"That money is mine, and these two goons can do their worst to me, but remember something, I'm a trained spy. They taught me at Langley how to endure pain."

The woman sighed and spoke to the two men who came with her. "Get started."

Matthews was gagged by one man, as the other man lowered the blinds on the windows and checked to see that all the doors were locked. They were on a private island without another soul around for miles, but why take chances that someone might see them or walk in?

The woman watched as Matthews was beaten, and although she hated to admit it, it fascinated her.

She had expected the men to begin their torture of Matthews by breaking or severing Matthews' fingers or toes. Instead, after putting on gloves, they started pounding Matthews' face. A short time later, his features were covered in blood and appeared lopsided and swollen.

Matthews only lasted for about forty hard blows; the final six, the ones that broke his resolve, they were given after he had been revived with smelling salts.

It was quite a bit less punishment than the woman would have liked to see him suffer, but Matthews gave up the money, and so she ordered the men to cease beating him.

When the men confirmed that the money was where Matthews claimed it to be, they initiated a transfer of the funds into an account owned by the Burke Corporation.

The woman smirked as she looked down at Matthews. So much for all that bullshit about having been trained to withstand torture.

Although Matthews' face was a wreck, she figured that he might look normal again someday, what with all the advances that medical science had made in the field of plastic surgery.

As she was leaving, the woman assured Matthews that she would send medical help, then she gave him a bit of news.

"Expect more visitors. Your friends from Langley will be coming to speak to you. They figure that if you betrayed us, you may have betrayed them too."

After spitting out bloody chunks from several broken teeth, Matthews spoke in a hoarse voice.

"Never… I love my country."

The woman, former FBI agent Sara Blake, sent him a doubtful look.

"Goodbye, Matthews. You'd better hope that Tanner doesn't decide to pay you a visit of his own someday."

∽

CODY, WYOMING

AMY LAUGHED AFTER TOSSING A FRISBEE THAT BOUNCED off Scar's head, and as she made the throw, her diamond engagement ring sparkled in the sun.

After leaving Mexico, the Tin Horsemen flew to Oklahoma City and reclaimed their motorcycles from the gas station where they had left them in storage, and then rode to Spenser's house.

With Alvarado dead and everyone safe, Spenser decided to throw a party. Abrasion accompanied Amy to her store in town to bring back food and supplies, and that was where he met a young lady named Deedee, who worked for Amy at the store.

Deedee was twenty, blonde, and just loved motorcycles. By the time Abrasion left the store, his crush on Amy was over, and when Deedee came to the party, she and Abrasion were inseparable.

The boys hugged Spenser when he told them that the money given to Abrasion by Alvarado was theirs to keep. They had been hoping that Spenser might give them part of it, and to have the whole amount blew their minds.

They now had plans to buy new motorcycles. "Some big muthas," Scar said.

When Bruise suggested that they give a chunk of the money to Scar's mother, "You know, for all the food and shit she gave us since we moved in," the boys all agreed. Bruise also planned to see a dentist about his missing tooth.

Spenser picked up the Frisbee and handed it to Scar. "We have to go soon, Johnny, or Amy and I will miss our plane to New Orleans."

"Okay, and we should get on the road too. It's a long ride back home."

Amy walked over and they all looked out at the generator shed, where Abrasion was saying goodbye to Deedee.

"I really thought Lionel might stay in the area now that he's met Deedee," Amy said.

"Oh, we'll be back," Scar said. "We can't live with my

mom forever, and when I told her about the money, she said she might sell the house and move to Texas to be with my Aunt Patty, since my Uncle Bob died a few weeks ago."

Spenser didn't hear a word about Scar's mother, his Aunt Patty, or the recently deceased Uncle Bob, all he heard was that the Tin Horsemen were staying in Cody.

"You're all moving here?" Spenser said.

"Uh-huh, Deedee says her brother has a house for rent cheap, and hey dude, whenever you need help on a case, just let us know."

Amy saw the look on Spenser's face and laughed.

∽

TANNER LOADED A DUFFEL BAG INTO THE REAR OF ALEXA'S van, and then it was time to say goodbye.

Tanner had retrieved the van from the nearby airfield they had left it at when they'd flown to Texas.

He had come back to Wyoming alone, as Alexa wanted to spend time with Rodrigo and Emilio. She would be joining him in Los Angeles when her visit was done.

While Spenser and Amy were headed to New Orleans, Tanner was taking Alexa to Hawaii, where the two of them would relax and figure out what came next.

As Amy stood by watching, the two Tanners shared a hug, as they prepared to part from each other.

"I'm not sure that I could have killed Alvarado without you, Spenser," Tanner said.

As the hug ended, Spenser looked at Tanner while smiling. "Since when do you doubt yourself?"

"I'll always be your apprentice, and I've learned from you once again."

Spenser gave him a serious look, and there was a gleam of pride in his eyes.

"Who are you?"

Cody Parker stood just a little straighter as he gave the answer to that question.

"I'm Tanner."

The grin came back to Spenser's face.

"You're goddamn right you are."

TANNER RETURNS!

OCCUPATION: DEATH - BOOK 12

AFTERWORD

Thank you,

REMINGTON KANE

JOIN MY INNER CIRCLE

You'll receive FREE books, such as,

SLAY BELLS – A TANNER NOVEL – BOOK 0

TAKEN! ALPHABET SERIES – 26 ORIGINAL TAKEN! TALES

BLUE STEELE - KARMA

Also – Exclusive short stories featuring TANNER, along with other books.

TO BECOME AN INNER CIRCLE MEMBER, GO TO:
   http://remingtonkane.com/mailing-list/

TANNER TIMES TWO
Copyright © REMINGTON KANE, 2015
YEAR ZERO PUBLISHING

This book is a work of fiction. Names, characters, places and incidents either are products of the author's imagination or are used fictitiously.

Any resemblance to actual events or locales or persons, living or dead, is entirely coincidental.

All rights reserved. Except as permitted under the U.S. Copyright Act of 1976, no part of this publication may be reproduced, distributed or transmitted in any form or by any means, or stored in a database or retrieval system, without the prior written permission of the publisher.

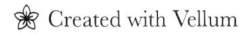

❦ Created with Vellum

Printed in Great Britain
by Amazon